A WALK IN THE PARK

SVEN LUNDIN

Ballast Books, LLC
www.ballastbooks.com

ISBN 978-1-964934-53-2 (Paperback)
ISBN 978-1-964934-54-9 (Ebook)

Printed in the United States of America

Published by Ballast Books
www.ballastbooks.com

For more information, bulk orders, appearances, or speaking requests, please email: info@ballastbooks.com.

Chapter 1

It was Saturday, mid-March, in Denver, Colorado, a clear day with warming sun and a temperature in the mid-sixties. Tomorrow, winter and snow were again in the forecast, but today was a day to enjoy. Alex Donner was relaxing on a bench at the playground, face in the sun and an eye on his grandson Michael (which, of course, nobody called him). The youngster was full of energy, like all the kids, running around the many slides and climbing contraptions, around and around, up and down, never slowing or stopping.

Mike was dressed in a pair of bright red sweatpants, easy to spot among the kids. Alex had come down from Breckenridge to spend the weekend with his daughter Mary and his grandson, who was five years old, tall for his age, and already in preschool. Mary's husband, Frank, had just left on a two-week business trip to Europe.

Alex's weekend visits had become a little tradition, partly to spend time with his family, partly to escape the ski area with its unbearable weekend crowds. His two daughters, their husbands, and their children were the family he had after he lost his wife in a car accident eight years ago. He had come to enjoy his independence and after retirement had relocated to his favorite mountain town.

Time in retirement exceeded Alex's expectations by a long shot. He finally had time for his interests, which had been suppressed over many years in an interesting but time-consuming career as an international security specialist, initially in cybersecurity for government and financial institutions and later spilling over into personal and property security for high-net-worth individuals.

And now, all his concerns were how to dress in the morning to pursue his interests—golf, biking, and hiking in the summer, downhill and cross-country skiing in the winter, and then the occasional sailing escapades with old buddies in different parts of the world. And on top of it all, he finally had time for his family with a growing number of grandchildren.

The sharp sound of gunshots popped his daydream and had people screaming and running in all directions, trying to find their kids and shelter. Alex jumped up, looking for Mike. After a few seconds, he got the shock of his life. Two bright red, kicking legs were sticking out from under the arms of a man walking very quickly away from the playground. Before his brain had time to react, Alex was running like a maniac, oblivious to anything and anybody in his way. He was closing in, but still some distance away, when he saw a car parked on the grass. The rear door was swung open by somebody inside.

The man was ready to dive in. There, it looked like something went wrong. The man's attempt to quickly get inside was slowed down, maybe by Mike's kicking. Instead of getting in after the kid, he stood up, ready to close the door from the outside.

That's when Alex took the last step before reaching his target. He was thirty years past his prime but stayed in good shape. It was a six-foot, two-hundred-pound body slamming into the unprepared man. Right knee in the soft middle, left elbow hitting the head. The man's head got wedged between the door and the B-pillar, his body slumped. Alex had Mike out in a couple of seconds.

A woman in the driver's seat was screaming something about abandoned children. She was in a police uniform. Her attempt to open the door was not successful. She would have to break the man's neck to get out or crawl over to the other side. Either way, she was slowed down enough to lose the opportunity to use her gun to stop Alex.

Alex was running along a parkway with Mike in his arms. Weekenders were still in shock and didn't pay any attention; just another frightened parent.

He was running toward a restroom building. There, he would be out of sight of both the car and the playground and could check on Mike. The smell of chloroform was strong, and the kid was in some sort of daze, maybe bordering on unconscious. Despite what had happened, he was not physically hurt. In the restroom, Alex washed Mike's face with cold water, which he didn't like much, but it woke him up. He vomited immediately and started to cry. Alex opened a bottle of water that he always carried, while also holding and comforting his grandson. He flushed water into Mike's mouth and over his face. That helped. Mike's crying stopped, and he looked up at his grandfather with a worried face. Alex tried to comfort him.

"You got something bad in your mouth, Mike, but now I think it's all out and you will soon feel fine again. Let's go home to Mommy so you can rest a little."

Mike didn't protest. They left the restroom and started to walk, Mike still in Alex's arms. After a couple of minutes, Mike said he could walk by himself, but that was not quite true, and Alex picked him up again. After a few minutes, they tried to walk hand in hand. It lasted a minute. To Alex, the walk was painfully slow. They heard nothing from the policewoman in the car, but they could now hear both police and ambulance sirens. Alex had not seen any familiar faces around the playground or the walking path, mainly just young parents with their children. Maybe some kids recognized Mike, but hopefully, nobody knew where he lived.

The walk home took about twenty minutes. When they got there, Alex's plan for the next few days was ready. Max, the black Lab and whatever mix, came running like a torpedo but slowed down in puzzlement when he smelled the lingering chloroform and saw Mike's sad expression and Alex's serious face.

Mary was surprised by their early return. Maybe her son had scratched his knee? But looking more closely at Mike, she realized that something more serious was going on. She looked at Alex for an explanation. Alex ignored her unspoken question and asked Mike if he wanted some ice cream. His answer was both a yes and a smile. Mary got the message. She took Mike into the kitchen and scooped up a bowl of his favorite flavor. That was what he needed to both feel and look normal. She walked back to Alex, who was now in her office and out of earshot of Mike. Alex cut to the chase, as usual when he was serious and focused.

"Mike was playing with a bunch of kids. They were all running around, having a good time. I was sitting in the sun on a bench by myself. Suddenly, I heard gunshots and jumped up to look for Mike. Already the second pop made me realize it was firecrackers. I still looked for Mike to make sure he was OK and had not been run down in the chaos that followed. That's when I saw his red pants under the arm of this guy walking fast away from the playground. I ran after him and caught up just as he stood to close the door of a car he had put Mike in. He hadn't looked back yet, so he was unprepared for the tackle and ended up with his head wedged between the door and the B-pillar.

"I got Mike out and saw the driver was a woman in a cop uniform. I smelled chloroform, so I guess they tried to sedate Mike. The man was in plain clothes and looked middle aged. He didn't move. The woman was hysterical. I think she babbled something about abandoned kids. She also looked middle age. She tried to open the door but couldn't get it past the guy's head. Lucky for us, we got the minute we needed to get away. The firecrackers were clearly a distraction. They did not sound like real shots, but they were loud enough to shock people and create chaos.

"I ran with Mike to get out of sight. We went to a restroom where I could check him and get the chloroform off him. He vomited quite a bit, and I washed his mouth and face. After a moment he seemed fine. Kid is a trooper. But the strange thing here is the cop uniform. It's not good, not good at all. If the cops are on the wrong side here, I don't want to be in their custody and interrogated by them—end up dead in a lousy cell. Suicide, of course, admission of guilt, case closed.

"And if they *are* cops, they'll track us down in a few hours with a door-to-door search. We all need to leave the house as soon as possible. You, Mike, and Max should go to your sister's. Mike loves to play with his cousins. That should help him get over this ordeal.

"I'll take a ski trip in the mountains and follow the news till things clear and we know who, why, and what. It could take some time, so I'll visit some stores and get a few things. Then I'll drive home and go out to dinner and hopefully meet some buddies. Tell them I skied all day and skinned up for exercise. It'll be a good alibi in case it's needed.

"You and I should talk on the phone tonight and tomorrow. Talk about Mike and his stomach in case somebody is listening in. I hope to leave the city before the storm moves in this evening. I plan to leave my house tomorrow night and spend a few weeks in the woods. We should have a good snowstorm by then—my kind of vacation."

Alex smiled. Mary did not. But she grasped the severity of the situation and was ready to call her sister with some lame excuse for the sudden visit. They would all be off in a matter of minutes: Mary, Mike, and Max to her sister Ellie in Evergreen, forty-five minutes away; Alex on his shopping spree. It was also agreed that Alex would turn off his cell phone when he left his house for the woods. Alex hugged them and was off.

The shopping was uneventful. Alex took time to visit a few stores to reduce his chances of being remembered. He got a Norwegian ski pulk, camo tent, sub-freezing sleeping bag, a month's supply of freeze-dried food, propane cans, and some clothing and survival things he might need. He also visited a hardware store and bought a couple of hoisting blocks and one hundred feet of quarter-inch rope.

It was late afternoon when he was done and headed up the mountains. The interstate traffic was light, as were the snow flurries. All the same, he maintained the speed limit plus about five. He was relaxing, finally, after his nice walk in the park—which turned out anything but. He now had an hour to ponder his situation, plan for tomorrow, and listen to the news. He had resisted the temptation all afternoon to focus on the task at hand.

The news was confusing. A radio station had interviewed some of the parents and older kids who had been at the park. Common to all was that the day was completely normal, fun, and nice, with everyone having a good time. Most of the kids knew or recognized each other. There were no strangers around.

Then gunshots had been fired, and people had panicked and run in all directions. It was complete chaos. The gunshots were later found to be firecrackers. Nobody knew who had set them off. It was a disgusting prank.

A couple of witnesses who had been close to the police-woman had heard her mention abandoned children in an incoherent way.

One couple, a young air force captain and his wife, who were playing with their two-year-old child on the grass outside the playground, had seen a middle-aged man coming from the playground and walking fast at the same time the firecrackers went off. He carried a child with bright red pants under his arm and was heading toward a car parked on the grass.

An elderly man ran after him and tackled him very hard just when he stood up to close the door. The man quickly got the child out and disappeared. The man who got tackled looked bad, hanging with his neck jammed between the door and the B-pillar.

Contact with the local chief of police, Andrew Walker, added to the confusion. There was no explanation for the police officer's presence at the playground. The identity of the man in her company was unknown. He confirmed that talks were ongoing within the police department, here and around the country, on how to identify high-risk kids and save them from ending up in gangs and lives in crime. The target group was ten- to sixteen-year-old children living or hanging out on the streets. So far nothing had been decided, and the talks certainly did not include preschoolers. An internal investigation was underway. In the meantime, the chief urged the man who disappeared with the child to come forward and help clarify the situation.

Alex was relieved. They had not found his or Mike's identities, so they had no clue who to look for. At least, not at this point.

As he drove up the mountain range, the snow intensified. By the time he got through the Eisenhower Tunnel, it was close to whiteout. The road was almost empty. He drove at crawling speed with an eye on the left barrier. That would be his driving mode for the long downslope until he left the interstate and turned onto the road to Breckenridge.

The Land Cruiser behaved as always. With its four-wheel drive and heavy-duty snow tires, it was the safest transportation in this weather. As he drove through Frisco, his mood was lifted from all the lights inside homes and businesses. The town looked warm and inviting in the snowstorm. Another half hour and he would be home. It was already past six; he would have to park the car and walk straight to the restaurant for dinner. Hopefully, some of his buddies would be there.

By seven o'clock, he had his drink at the bar, exchanging words of wisdom with patrons he knew, some well. He needed witnesses. *What had he been up to today?* He skinned up to twelve thousand feet in the morning, skied home, had lunch, and took a nap. For almost three hours. *Had he heard about the cop who got beat up at a playground in Denver?* Very briefly. What was going on? *A messy situation. It's unclear why the cops were there in the first place and why a kid was picked up. A man presumed to be his grandfather got the kid back and just disappeared. Almost killed the guy who picked the kid up. Crazy.*

The food showed up. Alex had a glass of his favorite cabernet and found the steak even more delicious than usual. Even this tumultuous day was suddenly quite agreeable.

Back at the house, he sat down to review the situation with an eye on the TV and an open fire going. He would have to wait for the late news to get an update but decided against it and turned off the TV. He would get all the news in the morning. Most important now was to plan tomorrow and the near future so he could survive a few weeks in the wild and hopefully find out from the news what the hell was going on. And how exposed his family was. And who was behind it all. But now, he needed sleep. Tomorrow morning would begin a twenty-four-hour workday, at least.

Alex woke up to a cold, snowy, and windy Sunday morning. He made himself his favorite breakfast: a couple of eggs, bacon, toast, juice, and a bucket of coffee. It could be weeks till the next one. He turned on the TV at seven. The main news was that the man who had picked up a child at a playground and then been attacked by a presumed relative to the child had died from his injuries. It was still not clear if the dead man was a police officer.

Law enforcement urged the attacker to come forward and help sort out this tragedy and clear his name. They had now, through eyewitnesses and the force and speed of the attack, come up with a sketch of the wanted man. He was a white male in his late forties or early fifties, six foot two, 220 pounds, well trained, possibly ex-military, and possibly a grandfather—or worst case, a kidnapper.

The adrenaline pushed Alex to go through his morning warmup routine with added weights and longer stretches. He worked up a good sweat and finished with a cold shower. Better get used to it. He dressed lightly for the morning packing.

First, he pulled the five-foot ski pulk from the Land Cruiser and put it on his workbench. He stowed his heavy gear at the bottom; food and cooking equipment in the back; sleeping bag, clothing, and footwear up front; and finally his large camo backpack with tent, shotgun, first aid kit, binoculars, headlamp, compass, rope, and blocks on top. He strapped it all down under its cover. It was now over a hundred pounds of supply he hauled into the Land Cruiser. Finally, he put in his mountain skis, with skins and poles. It was almost noon.

Alex had again gotten into a sweat and went back for a second shower, this time hot and long. He needed to go through his plan for the day and look for oversights. The snowstorm was still intense. It should go on for another night and day. Snowplows were out and the roads were barely passable. Could he make it to Frisco and back, and then to Frisco again, all after nightfall? Would buses run in this weather? If it didn't work, the whole plan had to be pushed off till tomorrow—not what he wanted. The bad weather was his ally, his cover, and it might end tomorrow. He had to try to go tonight. Worst case, he would leave the Land Cruiser in Frisco, by the bus station.

He decided to call Mary and find out how Mike was doing, to see if he had overcome his horrible ordeal from yesterday. He also wanted to create another smoke screen and had come up with a story about dinner this evening with his friend Don, all for the benefit of anybody who thought about checking his phone. He was confident his daughter would catch on and play along. Mary picked up on the second ring.

"Hi, Dad, did you get home without any problem yesterday?"

"Yes, of course. This is what my car is built for. And how's my favorite grandson feeling today? Is his stomach better?"

"He's doing just fine. Whatever he had took care of itself. Did you hear what happened yesterday at a playground close to our house?"

"Well, yes. It was awful. Either a father or grandfather who retrieved a kidnapped child, or a kidnapper who killed a cop to grab a child. Either way is weird. Whenever we get the whole story, it may be something totally different. Thank God you and Mike were out of town."

"Oh yes, that was a blessing. Do you have any dinner plans tonight?"

"As a matter of fact, I do. My buddy Don called and invited me. He said he had some business to discuss. I told him I was retired, but he brushed that away. Either way, his wines and Joanne's cooking are worth putting up with whatever he has come up with."

"Well, enjoy the evening, and call me later and let me know what happened?"

"Will do. Say hi to all and have a nice dinner."

"I'll do that. Bye, Dad."

Alex made lunch and watched the news; there was nothing surprising or new. It was early afternoon. He planned to leave at six, so it was time for an hour's rest and to search for holes in his plan. By four, he started to get dressed, slowly and methodically, considering all possible situations he might get into and how to deal with them. He was going to carry a small backpack with water, energy bars, a headlamp, and some extra gloves. He needed to carry that backpack on the bus to Frisco. He would look suspicious without one on a bus late at night, supposedly going home from work.

At dusk, he left. There was a lull in the storm, but only a lull. The storm would keep up till midday tomorrow. Drifting snow made driving slow. Sliding off the road would be the end of his entire plan. At fifteen miles per hour, he moved through town down the highway toward Frisco. No cars, just snowplows and a couple of cop cars. To his delight, he met a bus halfway to Frisco.

In town, he turned left on Main Street, drove to the western intersection, and got on the interstate. It was the same as the town—a few snowplows and trucks, but no cars. As he got close to Officers Gulch, he got prepared to exit the interstate if the ramps were plowed. They were not, as he suspected. With no traffic in sight, he stopped the Land Cruiser, got out, and dumped the ski pulk over the railing and down into the deep snow pile below, just by the underpass. There, it should be safely buried until he got back. He drove west another mile and turned around at Copper Mountain.

When he got back to Frisco and turned off the interstate, he stopped at the first parking lot on his right. He got his skis and poles out and buried them in the deep snow. He then drove back home and into his garage. It was just about 9:30 p.m. and time to call his daughter. She immediately answered.

"Hi, Dad, did you have a nice dinner?"

"Yes, I did, and I'm glad I don't eat like that every day. I would push three hundred pounds now. How are all the kids doing? Are they sleeping yet?"

"Yes, they are, and the rest of us are about ready to do the same. They drain us. So, what did Don have to talk about?"

"Well, it was actually an interesting evening. We only talked business. I think you know Don is part owner of a large microchip company. My company designed and installed their security system several years ago. The majority owner has decided to overhaul and upgrade the system, including those in his two main homes in West Palm Beach and Aspen. Don showed me the new contract with one of our former competitors. The owner is happy with what we did, and he knows I am retired, but he wants me involved to oversee the project in whatever capacity I am agreeable to. He asked us both to come and join him on his yacht. Right now, it's docked in the Bahamas. His jet could pick us up tomorrow or the day after, weather permitting, in Denver or Aspen."

Mary listened with a smile. Was this the father she knew? The boring straight shooter who only believed in truth and honesty, now fabricating this incredible story in just a few hours to throw any potential eavesdropper off course.

"Oh, Dad, I thought you said you were retired. But I can see how going on a yacht trip is hard to turn down. Have lots of fun and say hi to Don."

They said goodbye, and Alex returned to reality. He got his backpack, activated the alarm, and set off toward the bus stop on foot. Would he find a bus to take him down to Frisco, or would he have to walk all the way? Walking would take four to five hours, plus possibly attention by some police car.

There were still buses running. He was relieved. The drive down to Frisco in almost whiteout conditions was slow. He got off at the marina bus stop and walked up Main Street through town, in strong wind and without seeing a soul. He reached his skis just after eleven o'clock. Around him was only wind, snow, and darkness. Perfect!

It took him an hour to ski up the bike path to the gulch and cross the interstate on the underpass. The pulk had landed in deep snow without any damage. He put on the harness and started to ski across the open field. He was not worried about being spotted; there were very few vehicles on the road, only trucks and snowplows, and all the drivers were staring at the road in close to zero visibility.

As he started his trek, he was careful not to work too hard. He did not want to break into a sweat; moist garments are poor insulators. The field he had to cross was well over a thousand feet, and if it took an hour or two was of no concern. Well across, he would follow the opening between the trees up into the woods and the gulch.

There, he would face an incline, and to move over a hundred pounds in deep snow would take its toll. His plan was to disconnect the pulk every half hour or so and ski in between the trees, looking for a campsite. There was always a possibility that some snowmobilers would come flying up the trail for fun in the morning. He would rather stay out of their way.

He found a spot that met his approval. It was level, not visible from the trail, and surrounded by trees. There was a short but quite steep incline to get there, so he took out the rope and pulled the pulk up without too much effort. After flattening the snow with his skis, he pulled out the tent. That's when he saw the first light of Monday morning. He had not checked the time since leaving the house last evening. The tent went up in a few minutes. Here, he would camp for the day, have a good meal, listen to the news, and sleep. His plan had worked without a hitch—so far.

After he finished eating, he crawled into the sleeping bag and was asleep before even reaching for the radio. When he woke up, it was already past three in the afternoon. He lit the stove for coffee, for heat, and for his meal. He got the radio out and turned it on. He found the frequencies, first for the news, then the police. The weather was going to clear, but only for a day or two. More snow was expected mid-week. There was little news about the event at the playground. The local radio only confirmed that the police had made no progress. That was all.

After eating and going through his routines, Alex got the maps out. He didn't know his exact position, but close enough to decide on a northwesterly direction. That should take him away from the trail that might be used by skiers or snowmobiles heading up towards the ski hut about a mile away. By the time he packed up and was ready to leave, daylight was just about gone, as were the storm clouds. He decided to ski away without the heavy pulk to find the next campsite. That should save him quite a bit of time.

As he started his trek, he was amazed, as many times before, how bright the night was, even without the moon, when the ground was snow-covered and the sky was clear. A billion stars lit up the world.

It all worked out well. He found a good spot, retrieved the pulk, and had the tent up and ready before daybreak. He settled in, cooked and ate his morning meal, and then went down to sleep.

It was two o'clock in the afternoon when he woke up and turned on the radio. No reception. As he contemplated this, he heard the soft sound of an engine. It could be an airplane, or a drone, or a snowmobile. The sound grew quickly. It was moving in his direction. Alex got out of the sleeping bag and into his clothes in no time. It was definitely a snowmobile. Maybe two. The noise was now very strong and very close. And then, suddenly, the engines were shut off. Alex still had to get his ski pants, boots, and parka on. He heard men talking. He got out of the tent and started to move toward the sound. The ground was flat, but the snow was deep, and after fifty feet or so, he had to move up a little hillside. Maybe just a berm or a snow pile that kept him out of view of the newcomers.

Suddenly, it got quiet, and he heard what sounded like a door closing. Eventually he saw the whole picture. Right in front of him was the ski hut, or rather log building, maybe a hundred feet away. In front were two snowmobiles with *Sheriff* painted on them. The two deputies were inside the building. If he had arrived during daylight, he would probably have seen the roof of the building between some trees, but in the dark it had not been visible.

Before his brain had processed what he saw, Alex felt his heart rate build. He went back to the tent and assembled and loaded his shotgun, just in case. He got the binoculars and moved back toward his lookout. He looked for some bushes to hide behind. There were three tiny spruce saplings about ten feet to the right of his first lookout. Perfect cover! He could see the deputies, but with his camo hood up, he would be invisible to them.

There he waited. After a few minutes, smoke started to exit the chimney. They were lighting a fire, maybe planning to stay overnight.

As Alex tried to come up with a plan, the front door opened, and the men came out. One coughed hard. They must have had problems getting the fire going. The room had gotten smoky and now they had come out for fresh air. But not only that. One had a bottle in his hand, and they both carried guns, one a shotgun and the other a sniper rifle. They both took a swig of whatever was inside the bottle. They laughed, slapped each other's backs, and had another swig.

From their noisy conversation, this was not their first taste of what was in the bottle. But that was not as interesting as the topic of their conversation—because *Alex* was the topic. And not in a way that made him want to join the party.

"There is no way the guy has a chance. Even if the media has declared him innocent, and even if that cop paid the ultimate price for her stupidity, they could never get to all the cops involved," one deputy said.

The other added, "Right. The first guy to spot him will shoot to kill. In self-defense, of course. $200,000 is more than enough to guarantee his death. Sure, we don't know his identity yet, but that's only a matter of time. There were enough people at that playground to recognize him and make him a local hero. Then *pop*, and it's business as usual."

Alex listened in disbelief. It was clear they were talking about the attack at the playground over eighty miles away, and there was a huge prize on his head. He had stepped on a hornet's nest of corrupt law enforcement, and he could only think of one thing: regardless of guilt or innocence, he was a dead man.

The man with the bottle put it down on the entrance steps, and both deputies cocked their guns. *Not for target shooting, that's for sure.* They started to shoot into the woods, laughing when a branch came down or a small tree fell over. Then they started to rotate for fresh targets in the fading light.

Their rotation brought both bullets and pellets closer to Alex's location. And he was not ready to get killed by those thugs, not now, not ever. They might not even know if they shot him, and the thought that they might not collect the prize money didn't make him feel any better.

Alex aimed his shotgun through one of the tiny saplings in preparation. Maybe the senseless shooting would stop! But that didn't happen. When the sniper rifle was pointed in his direction, he fired.

The deputy with the shotgun froze where he stood. He could not comprehend what had happened. Had the rifle exploded? He bent down over his dead buddy in total shock. He talked to him. He checked the rifle. He cried. Finally, he looked up in Alex's direction, looking for a ghost. Alex was now standing up. He was the last thing the man saw.

Alex looked at the two bodies lying in the snow. To their right were two snowmobiles with *Sheriff* painted on them, to their left was a large log building, and in the background was a beautiful, wooded mountain terrain. The snow around their bodies was slowly turning crimson red. Alex felt divided. On one hand, two human beings with good lives and futures as law enforcement officers had had their lives cut short by him. On the other hand, they had sworn to obey the Constitution and then had joined an entity whose purpose was to steal and sell young, defenseless children for a pitiful monetary gain. And his grandson had been one of their targets. He clenched his fist and turned around.

Alex returned to the campsite and packed his gear in the pulk. There was new snow falling, which hopefully would cover his tracks whenever somebody found the bodies.

Chapter 2

Linda Crawford and her husband, Mark, were having a late Saturday lunch at their suburban home. The TV was on in the background. Linda suddenly stopped eating when the incident at the playground was broadcast. "Did you hear that?" she asked her husband, a law professor at the nearby University of Denver. He affirmed he had. "Do you think I should check it out?"

"You have to. It fits the parameters of your assignment."

Special Agent Linda Crawford was a twenty-three-year veteran at the Denver FBI office. Two weeks ago, the special agent in charge of the Denver office, Tom Baker, had given Linda the task of investigating several disturbing occurrences of lost children, all in the northwestern US.

Over about five months, there had been seven children abducted—girls and boys, all four and five years old, all white, and all from middle-class families. Similarities between all the abductions were no witnesses, no random notes, no bodies, and no closures for the families, who were tortured by grief and lack of answers.

Linda had started her new assignment by studying the details of each of the disappearances. They were all similar, in as much as they had happened in broad daylight in middle-class neighborhoods with people around, and yet no witnesses and no traces.

Linda's conclusions were that there must have been several people involved who helped create distractions. Maybe clowns, or jugglers, or people arguing. To be so successful, they must have been well planned. They were definitely not random. The geographic spread pointed toward a substantial organization, most likely with lots of money at hand. That would suggest they did other things besides kidnapping, like prostitution, human trafficking, and drug smuggling. Kidnapping for money, possibly to order, was her conclusion.

That's why immediately after their lunch, Linda contacted the chief of the local police, Andrew Walker. She explained the reason for her call: that the FBI had gathered data from several kidnappings in the northwestern US, and it was her job to follow up on all cases to try and find any possible connections between them.

Chief Walker, like most police officers, sounded less than enthusiastic about a call from the FBI but was smart enough to invite her to his office Monday morning. She would then get a copy of the full report. Right now, he and his staff were busy trying to sort out what had happened, who the unidentified man in the company of the police officer was, and what they were doing at the playground. At this point, there was nothing he could add.

The next call was to the largest of the news stations that had been at the crime scene. Linda introduced herself and asked that a transcript of the entire story, the interviews, and also material not included in the broadcast be emailed to her.

This was not an unusual request by law enforcement, and the substantial email arrived less than an hour later. The most interesting part was an interview with an air force captain, Larry Simpson. Linda immediately contacted the air force base in Colorado Springs and, after a couple of minutes, got his contact number. She got Captain Simpson on the line.

"Captain Simpson, my name is Linda Crawford. I am a special agent with the FBI here in Denver. I am calling regarding the disturbance at a playground in Littleton earlier today. From the news coverage, I understand you witnessed all or part of that occurrence. What happened has similarities with several kidnappings in the northwestern US over a five-month period. Seven children, four and five years old, have been abducted and disappeared without a trace. I would appreciate it if I could have an hour of your time this afternoon. I can come over to your home, or we can meet at any place you would prefer. Would that work for you?"

Captain Simpson's response was immediate. "Of course we can meet. I'm here with my family visiting my wife's parents in Littleton. You're welcome here; I'm sure we can find a room to sit and talk."

Linda arrived half an hour later. She greeted the whole family before Captain Simpson and his wife led her into a comfortable home office.

"First, I appreciate your time, and I will try to make this as short as possible. Also, for the record, this conversation is being recorded," Linda started. "The seven abductions I mentioned have several things in common. They all happened in broad daylight, in public places, involving white, middle-class children. There have been no ransom notes, no traces, and no witnesses, and there has always been some kind of distraction. Today's incident follows the same pattern, except for the witness part. You two are among the first eyewitnesses to what could have been the eighth abduction. That's a short summary so that you can appreciate why I needed to talk to you.

"About today's event, can you go through what you saw today? Give me every little detail, including the gunshots and the distraction."

Both thought for a moment, and then Captain Simpson said, "First of all, we will be very happy if we can help, any time. What you just told us hits right home. We have a two-year-old girl, and I cannot imagine what it would feel like for a parent to face the situation you described. You got my adrenaline pumping, and I'll try to remember every detail.

"We were sitting on the grass, playing with our daughter, maybe a hundred feet outside the playground. When I first heard a shot, I was alerted instantly. The second shot made me realize it was fireworks, not gunshots, and there were maybe six of them. So, we relaxed again, but I kept an eye on the playground to see if there were any rough kids around. That's when I saw this man come walking fast. He got my attention by the way he carried the kid under his arm, like a piece of luggage. Not very parentlike. I thought the kid must have misbehaved or something.

"Before I could think much about it, I saw this other guy come running. He ran very fast, and what got me was that he wasn't young. He looked about fifty or so but ran like a twenty-year-old. And without slowing down, he ran right into the man who had carried the child to a car and was now standing up to close the door. I thought they both would lie on the ground after that collision, but that didn't happen. The first guy's head got stuck between the door and the B-pillar, and the runner had the child out in a second and just kept going.

"My instinct was to run up and check the guy hanging from the car, but with all the running and chaos, I decided against it. I couldn't leave my wife and daughter exposed. After a few moments, I also saw a policewoman get out of the car on the passenger side, which of course added to the confusion. I tried to make some sense of it all, and the only thing I could come up with was that the runner was a father or a grandfather, and the guy that was tackled had grabbed the child. I didn't even think about kidnapping—more like a custody dispute. But one thing is clear in my mind: The runner is a relative who saved the child. Nobody else could run and tackle like that, with such passion and fury.

"That's what I remember, and also that the kid had very bright red pants. The man who saved him had no hat, grayish hair, a short, gray jacket, and dark pants."

After a moment, Captain Simpson's wife said: "I don't have much to add. When the shooting started, I immediately grabbed our baby and checked her. Larry told me right away that it was fireworks, so I relaxed. I saw what he saw, and I agree with him: The man who came running was a blood relative. No other person could be so passionate. I really hope you find the other children, and if we can help in any way, we will."

There was a moment before Linda spoke.

"That was very helpful, particularly when you said that the elderly man, the runner, was a relative who saved the child and not a stranger who abducted him. Only by being there and seeing the whole thing could you have come to that conclusion. That is very important when we decide our next step. You've already helped us more than I had hoped. I don't need to take more of your time, but I may have more questions, and I hope I can call you again. And if you think of something else, please give me a call."

They stood up and exchanged business cards. Captain Simpson assured her they would call if something else came to mind.

Half an hour later, Linda was back home. She found Mark in the kitchen and gave him a long and silent hug. Mark broke the silence. "It's that bad?"

"Yes, and maybe worse. I feel certain the police are involved, one way or another."

Mark took a step back and looked at his wife.

"Now that's a huge conclusion after one interview. Tell me what you found out."

Her husband took in every word and waited till the end before asking his very pointed questions. Then he concluded, "I agree with you. But remember, it's all circumstantial. Until you have proof, you can't do anything but play along. And hiding your suspicion may lead them to make a mistake. Now, do you know it's already past six, and we haven't even thought about dinner?"

Linda jumped up, kissed Mark on his forehead, and thanked him.

"I bought some sushi this morning. Can you survive on that?"

Mark said he could and started to mix a couple of martinis, very dry, with blue cheese olives. After a somewhat chaotic day, they finally could relax and have an enjoyable evening together.

The next day, on a cold, windy, and snowy Sunday morning, Linda woke up just after six. She sneaked out of bed without waking Mark and went down to the kitchen. She made herself a smoothie and walked into the living room to drink and think. It didn't take many minutes to come up with her next step, but she needed her boss's approval, and she couldn't call him for a few hours. So, she would have time for a long workout, a good breakfast, and a talk with Mark. A perfect Sunday morning!

They had their breakfast at eight on Sunday mornings. Mark came down well before that, having missed his wife in bed. They made breakfast together, as usual, and sat down. Mark commented on Linda's early rise and hoped she had slept well. She said she had and that she'd come downstairs for an early workout, a good way to clear her head.

"So, what have you decided?" Mark asked.

"As I see it," Linda started, "our first move ought to be to reduce the complexity of this mess by clearing the officer's name. She's the only known entity here. That means we need to get her work records, computers, and phone log—in other words, treat her as a suspect. And we must start as soon as possible, hopefully this afternoon. What do you think?"

Mark couldn't suppress a smile. "We're a little sneaky this morning, aren't we? But seriously, that's a pretty bold move. Calling the bluff right off the bat."

"Well, I still have to get the go-ahead from Tom. He also has to give me some backup. At least one additional guy."

By ten o'clock, Linda called her boss. Tom was in high spirits; he had been out jogging in the snowstorm and hadn't gotten any news so far. Linda told him she would ruin his weekend and needed an hour of his time.

"When?" he asked.

"Now," she answered.

"Come over," he said.

Linda got in her car and drove the few miles to her boss's house. His wife, Sandra, opened the door with her normal warm greeting, hoping it wasn't any bad news. Linda gave her a smile back without saying anything. Tom met her at the door and walked her into his study. Linda told him what had transpired in just a few minutes. He was a bright and experienced listener. He looked at her after she finished.

"I agree with your assessment and proposal. But this won't be easy for anyone, and you need help. I'll call Steve."

Without waiting for her comment, he picked up his phone and called his deputy.

"Steve, Tom here. Something damn delicate has come up. Can you come over to my house right now? Linda is here also. See you, bye."

While they waited, Tom went over to his desk and pulled out some documents. He looked them over and filled in some blanks.

Steve Callahan, a senior agent and Tom's deputy, showed up twenty minutes later. They all sat down in Tom's study, and Linda was asked to tell them what was going on. She did so, with an emphasis on the fact that witnesses to the entire event—parents, grandparents, a couple of children, an air force captain and his wife, who Linda had personally interviewed— had a totally different description of the occurrence than the policewoman.

In addition, the policewoman had been sitting in a car parked on the grass, partly hidden behind some trees and bushes. She did not have a clear view of the playground. Against that background, and the fact that nobody had any idea where to find the fifty-year-old man, in Linda's view, there was a good reason to remove any suspicion that the police officer was on the wrong side. This would require a visit to her office and home to secure evidence, and it should be done right away. Linda went silent and waited.

Finally, the deputy broke the silence.

"I'm with you, Linda. It's your case. But we need some papers."

Tom, who had been sitting at his desk and not said a word since Linda started talking, stood up and walked over. "Yes, you need these. Good luck!"

Steve and Linda drove to the local police headquarters. It was Sunday, but the urgency caused by the previous day's event meant that the entire office was up and running. They entered at 12:40 p.m., having passed a number of shivering news reporters up front. They went straight to the chief's office and told the secretary it was important that they could see him right away. She looked shell-shocked, but their demeanor got her out of her chair without a word. She walked to the door, knocked, and opened it. They heard the chief curse, telling her he would not see anybody; he was swamped with work.

Steve walked past her into the room, showed his credentials and search warrant, and said matter-of-factly: "Chief Walker, this is the FBI. We've been studying a number of kidnappings across the northwestern states over the last five months. Yesterday's attempt follows the same pattern as all the previous ones. We ask for your cooperation to pick up records, telephones, and computers belonging to the officer who was involved in the incident yesterday. This is to clear her name since there were conflicting statements from several witnesses. Will you please take us to her desk and ask your secretary to write down her address? Also, we need any information you have about the man in her company, his relation to the police department, and the claim that they were looking for high-risk children."

Chief Walker looked tired as he answered.

"The man in the officer's company died earlier this morning. I don't know who he is and why they were at the playground. Regarding high-risk children, we are talking about what we can do to identify them and save them from a life in crime. The target group is ten to sixteen-year-old children living on the streets. At this point, nothing has been decided, and our target group certainly does not include preschoolers."

Linda thanked him for the clarifications, and the two of them followed the secretary to the officer's desk. They got her home address and picked up her computer and telephone log. Nothing else of interest was found.

Linda and Steve left the police headquarters and drove to the woman's home. A middle-aged man opened the door when they knocked. Linda introduced them and informed the man of the reason for their visit. The man told them his wife was out working. Linda and Steve walked through the house and secured a computer. They thanked the man and left.

Back at the office, they handed the computers and telephone log to a woman in charge of a small group that specialized in electronic forensic work. The group consisted of five highly skilled experts who had been called to duty when Linda and Steve left for their searches. They got a briefing on what to look for and instructions to call Linda whenever something interesting or suspicious caught their eye. It was just past five on Sunday afternoon. It would take several hours, maybe all night, before they had any results—if they found anything at all. Steve and Linda both had families, and with nothing more to do at this point, they both left for their respective homes.

The call came at 4:20 on Monday morning. Linda jumped out of bed and was on her way in fifteen minutes. The report was disturbing. There had been communication from the sheriff's office in Eagle County, in the western part of the state more than 120 miles away, to the female officer. The incoming message, received last Thursday, stated the need "to expedite delivery of requested item no later than coming Monday." The immediate response: "Understood." Nothing else. Still, it raised a red flag and called for an explanation. Linda went to the coffee machine, then to her office, and sat down to think. Just before six, she called Steve and presented the findings and her proposed next step.

"I think we should go back to the house, wake her up, and ask for a detailed explanation of the findings. What exactly is the 'item' that will be delivered on Monday, i.e., today? If she doesn't come up with an explanation that we can verify, we'll bring her to the office for further questioning. There, we will explain our suspicion and make her two choices clear: Do the right thing and cooperate or go to prison."

Steve had only one question: "And Tom's document covers this step?"

He didn't wait for an answer. He knew it did. A few minutes later, he was on his way to the office, where a cup of coffee was waiting.

They rang the doorbell at the female officer's house at seven o'clock in the morning. The officer had no explanation, first at home, then in the office. Her only response was: "I know nothing, and I want a lawyer."

Steve said, "That is not a wise response. But if that is your position, we will keep you here until a lawyer can be arranged."

No response.

At 8:30 a.m., the woman was transported to a holding cell in the building, and Steve and Linda were alone.

"The cop is involved. She's guilty as hell and scared to death," Linda started. "And there are seven other kids in this mess. What kind of people are behind all this?"

Steve nodded, deep in his own thoughts about the horrifying crime that they had just uncovered—or rather, that *Linda* had just uncovered. He asked Linda to call Tom. After all, it was her case, and she'd better get used to swinging the baton. Maybe for a long time.

Linda made the call to Tom. He listened, asked a few questions, and decided they should meet in his office right away.

After they sat down, Tom opened by saying, "The email came from another police district not even close to here. First, I have to call our director. He must decide on an investigation of the entire law enforcement organization in our state and who should be responsible for that. Maybe other states will get dragged in as well. At this point, the only thing we can do is to finish the female officer's hearing and then turn her over to the new investigative body. You have my instruction to go ahead with that."

Linda and Steve left Tom's office and went in and sat down in Steve's room just a few steps away. They were going to interrogate the female officer and needed to develop a plan. So far, she had not answered a single question. They had gone back and forth for a while before they finally decided to give in to her request for a lawyer. Did she have somebody she knew or had in mind? Maybe that would soften her up.

They walked down to the holding cell. The officer who oversaw it this morning said all was quiet. The lady had made no fuss and was sleeping. They opened the door with no reaction from the lady, and for a good reason—she was dead.

Linda turned white after Steve tried to wake her and discovered her situation. Steve's only comment was, "Why am I not surprised?"

They walked back to Tom's office and brought him the news. The coroner would come up with the cause of death, most likely cyanide or some other substance in a small pill, almost impossible to find in a normal body search.

"This is common in some international crime organizations, particularly those based in Russia and China. You screw up, you die," Tom added. "Those two made a big mistake, trying to rush an abduction by hitting a playground on a Saturday morning with no backup and inadequate distraction. They paid the price.

"We have learned a lot in three days. We're most likely dealing with an international organization based in Russia. As you said earlier, Linda, one of several ways to make money is kidnapping. Russian oligarchs would pay millions for a particular kid. You two have done a great job, and for you, Linda, there are still seven kids out there. We want to find them and bring them home."

Chapter 3

It didn't take Alex long to realize that the incline was too steep to pull the pulk tied to his body and make any meaningful progress. So, he unhooked the harness, pulled out the rope, and tied it around his waist. He then skied in a straight line as far as the rope and terrain would allow. It was then quite easy to pull the pulk up in the ski trail he had made. That routine would be repeated through the night. There would be at least two miles until he reached any leveled ground, and he would be happy to make one mile through the night.

The conversation between the two men indicated that the female police officer had died. How had that happened? She hadn't been touched in the turmoil. And what had happened to the guy he tackled? He didn't look so good, hanging from the door by his neck without moving or making any sound.

The night was uneventful with a steady snowfall. Soon after first light, Alex found a flat enough spot to camp for the day. He was tired after ten hours of constant short distances of skiing and working hard to pull his hundred-pound pulk, with only a few short breaks to drink some water and eat energy bars. The first thing he did after he got into the tent was light the stove and get the food kettle warmed up. After he got out of his ski gear, he got the radio and tried to find reception. No success, as expected. There were still some elevations blocking signals. Tomorrow should be better, higher up and closer to Copper Mountain.

Alex woke up at two in the afternoon. It was a cloudy day with light snow. With cloudy skies, the nights were dark, and it was hard to navigate, which had become obvious the previous night.

Also, from what he had heard the previous evening, there seemed to have been some development in the case that had removed him from the wanted list. The expected manhunt had not happened, but he was still on the death list among an unknown number of dirty cops. And the most important question remained: What would happen when the two bodies at the ski hut were found? That was enough reason to remain in hiding, but without air surveillance, there was no reason to hide all day and only move in the dark. Day skiing would make life on the lam a lot easier.

The following day was again cold and cloudy with light snow. Alex moved westward and tried to get higher up and out of the gulch he had followed so far. *That should help with radio reception.* He kept moving until late afternoon, when he came upon a nice flat spot, ideal for camping and with an open view southward. After settling in, he tried his radio and had a good reception. Finally, after three days of literal radio silence, he got all kinds of news: weather, traffic, politics, crimes, and finally, updates on the case he was involved in.

It was a rather lengthy report, which in summary said that the FBI, under the supervision of Special Agent Linda Crawford, was now involved because several unsolved kidnappings had happened over about half a year, all in northwestern US states. The female officer he saw in the driver's seat had died inside an FBI holding cell from a cyanide pill she had brought in a balloon hidden in a body cavity.

A task force involving several law enforcement agencies was being put together to investigate possible police corruption. The man who attacked the kidnapper last Saturday and retrieved a child was still not identified. He was not a suspect of any wrongdoing but wanted for questioning to help bring clarity to the case.

Alex laid back and stared at the canvas above his head. There was no talk about the two bodies at the hut. Were they still not discovered? He needed to move as far as possible before they were found. He also had a clear memory of their conversation about the number of officers involved.

The following couple of days were more of the same: clouds, snow, and some wind. Alex had now reached the point where he had decided to cross the interstate under two bridges built for creeks and wildlife. That had to be done at night, so he took a meal break and listened to the news.

The breaking news made him forget both food and time. It was with a solemn voice the reporter announced that two highly respected and decorated sheriff's deputies, who had been missing for two days, had been found dead. A close investigation had determined that it was an accident-suicide tragedy. One deputy had accidentally shot his colleague and close friend and then, in despair, ended his own life. No foul play was suspected, and the families asked for respect for their privacy at this very difficult time.

Alex was stunned. How was it possible to come to that conclusion? The entrance wound from a shotgun fired from around eighty feet had nothing in common with a suicide wound from less than a foot! He could only think of two explanations: Either some black bears or mountain lions had mutilated the bodies beyond any meaningful postmortem, or, more likely, the sheriff's office did not want any investigation, which would be closely followed by the media and the families of the deceased. They did not want questions about possible suspects and motives or calls from grieving family members and angry voters demanding answers and results. But behind the smoke screen, the hunt was on, and the prize on his head had taken a big jump.

The incredible news had totally made him forget the weather forecast, but that was a minor disadvantage. He decided that he should never think about this event, admit to it if questioned, or talk about it under any circumstances. In his own mind, it was a nightmare he would try to forget. He packed everything to be ready to leave as soon as darkness fell.

The night trek under the two bridges brought no surprises. The ground was fairly level, and he was well out of eyesight from the interstate already an hour before daybreak. He found a campsite and set up his tent. It had been one week since he set up his tent for the first time. He decided to go back to day skiing and stay where he was for about twenty-four hours. Some rest couldn't hurt.

The following morning, he woke up early and felt rested. He ate and packed his attire and was ready to start around eight. The first part was still uphill for about two hours. Then he came out onto a big, open, flat area with mountain ridges on the sides. He hugged the left side and moved close to the tree line. It would take him all day to cross the flat. On the other side, the land would start to drop, which would make his trekking a lot easier.

His plan was to ski in a southwesterly direction toward the Camp Hale National Monument. The distance was about eight miles as the crows fly and may take a week or more with ups and downs and around mountains. The entire trip would cross the training area for the elite soldiers of the Tenth Mountain

Division during World War II. He had thought about checking out the area for some time out of curiosity, and now it would happen.

From Camp Hale, he would continue to Leadville and then go back home. If the last leg was not skiable this late in the season, he would call a buddy or an Uber. His ski trip would last about three weeks from start to finish, just as planned. And more importantly, the events that were reported on the news pointed to a much bigger plot than what he had been part of. He was out of the picture.

At about two-thirds of the open area, there was a narrow, snow-covered road running into the woods. The snow was less than a foot deep, the whole valley having been windswept during the storm. There were car tracks on the road. Alex's eyes followed the tracks into the woods. He saw a building with a sign that read *Bed & Breakfast*, and beneath it, *Closed for the season*.

A woman came walking in his direction. There was no point trying to ignore her, so he took a break on the road, waiting. She was dressed in jeans, soft boots, a black down jacket, and a white furry hat. She stopped about thirty feet away. She looked to be in her mid-thirties, normal height and weight, white, average features, and no smile. She spoke with a firm voice and told Alex that the place was closed. Alex couldn't suppress a smile.

"I can understand that. This looks like a summer place, with lots of hikers around. And in any event, I carry my own B&B," he said, nodding toward his pulk. "So, are you here getting the place ready for the season?"

The woman seemed to relax. She took a few steps closer to Alex and looked at him with inquisitive eyes, like she was measuring him up and down. After she stopped about ten feet away, she spoke with a friendlier voice and a faint smile.

"You look like you've been out camping for a while. I'm just getting my dinner ready. Why don't you take a break and join me? You can even have a hot shower; I checked the power and the plumbing, and it all works. Then you can tell me your story. Come on in. I'm not as dangerous as I look."

Alex decided to accept the invitation. There was something that aroused his curiosity, even though he couldn't define it. They introduced themselves. She said her name was Kate.

As they got past the gate area with the sign, Alex got a full view of the building. It was two stories, with two windows on each side of the entrance door on the lower level and a large window above the entrance. On the second level, there was one dorm window on each side of the large window. It was an impressive and very attractive building.

There was a pickup truck parked to the left of the entrance, a gray Ford F-150 with a few years on it. The bed had extra sidings made from black and white painted planking. It looked like a farm truck for transporting hay, or sheep, or pigs.

Alex parked his pulk and skis beside the front entrance, got his backpack out from under the cover, dug out a roll of clothing, and followed the lady into the big house. Inside, the building continued to impress him. Its large hall or great room opened to a kitchen and dining area to the left and a huge sitting area with a big fireplace and pool table to the right. There were some rooms at the back of the building.

In the middle was a wide, straight staircase to the second level. It ended at a landing that ran the length of the big hall, then angled ninety degrees toward the front of the building. There were four doors along the back of the landing and one door on each side of it, all with what looked like small numberplates on them. The large window in the center flooded the whole inside of the building with light.

Alex removed his boots and followed the woman as she led him up the stairs to room number two, the left back corner room. As they entered, she said,

"This room is my favorite. It's sunny all day. We have six guest rooms and three Jack and Jill–style bathrooms. You don't have to worry; you have the whole floor to yourself. Dinner should be ready in about an hour, so take your time."

With that, she left, and Alex had time to wonder what was going on. She was too young to hit on him, and the place was a mansion. It had oak floors throughout and nice detailing and fixtures. There was a lot of money invested in this B&B.

He opened his backpack and started unpacking. First out were the binoculars, radio, knife, and toiletries, then some clothing and a box of ammo. Next, he got his shotgun pouch out, assembled and loaded the gun, and put it under the mattress. He had made a living preventing disasters, and old habits die hard.

He then started the shower, but before he undressed, he took a little tour of the adjacent bedroom. It was empty, as expected. The dorm window faced the road. He walked toward the door and listened. It was quiet. He carefully opened the door to peek out. There was nothing outside, but he heard the woman talking, probably on the phone. He took a step out onto the landing. She was in the kitchen just under him. Now he could hear her, although she talked in a hushed voice.

"Of course, I don't know for sure, but he meets all the descriptions we have, and the guys were shot about five miles from here. We just can't take any chances," she whispered. "No, no, he's quite pleasant . . . no, you have to come up and take care of it. I can't do it. You have till morning, but the sooner the better . . . OK, OK. I'll try that. OK, four would be perfect. Bye."

Alex hustled back into the bathroom. The water was now boiling hot, and he got it down to the right temperature. He washed his hair and body. It was his first shower in a week. He got out, dried himself, smiled, and felt good—actually, *very* good. He put on new underwear, lay down on the bed, stared at the ceiling, and tried to sort out his options.

First, he would go down and eat dinner with "Kate" (or whatever her real name was). It would most likely involve several glasses of wine, one with a pill in it—maybe a cyanide pill. But not in the first glass; it'd be too risky that the smell would alert him. Probably the third.

There was a simple solution to that problem—he didn't drink any alcohol, only water and coffee. He needed to stay awake all night anyway, so coffee would be his drink of choice. Besides, now his life depended on his own vigilance. He got up from the bed and put on a pair of jeans, a flannel shirt, and socks. They were all clean. That made him feel even better.

After about fifteen minutes of checking up the gun, ammo, and his hunting knife and putting everything in the right place for quick access, Alex went down to his hostess early to check that nothing unwanted ended up on his plate.

"Well, look at you! What a change. You look great," Kate greeted him.

"Thank you, and I feel great also. And thank you so much for inviting me. It made the day just wonderful, and the food smells fabulous as well. Now that I've found this little gem in the wilderness, I look forward to returning in the summer."

They both smiled. Kate offered him a glass of wine from a bottle she had just opened. He thanked her and explained that he did not drink alcohol and never had, but he would like a glass of water.

He got his water with ice and hung around the kitchen area, making small talk with his hostess but primarily checking every move she made. She was warming up some kind of stew of meat, potatoes, carrots, onions, mushrooms, beets, and other vegetables he couldn't identify. It smelled delicious after all the meals of freeze-dried food in his tent.

After about ten minutes, Kate decided the food had reached the desired temperature. She scooped up quite generous portions on two plates. Alex grabbed them and carried them to the table, then went back for the glasses—wine for her, water for him. He put them where he expected she wanted them. There were no protests, so he felt comfortable that he would survive the dinner.

After they were seated, Alex continued their small talk.

"I think I hear a faint East Coast accent. Are you from New England, maybe?" he asked.

"Yes, kind of," Kate responded. "I was born in Austria. My family moved to the Boston area when I was six years old. I've been here for thirty years now. Eleven years ago, I moved to Colorado, for skiing. The ski conditions here are quite different from New England. The mountains are higher and the snow drier. I'm a nurse by training, and I work as a ski patroller in Vail and Beaver Creek. At the end of the ski season, I do various jobs, like house-sitting for wealthy homeowners in the area and getting this B&B ready for the summer season."

"Interesting. And I guess you were too young when you left Austria to make a comparison between there and here."

"Yes, all I remember from back then are my grandparents. And you, what are you doing when you're not out skiing and camping? You look too young to be retired."

"Thanks for the compliment, but I'm retired five years already. If you think time flies when you're working, wait till you retire! Anyway, I was in the banking business. For the last ten years, I was the VP responsible for our platinum clientele. It allowed me—or forced me, depending on your point of view—to travel a lot and also experience lifestyles I could never dream of for myself even if I had wanted to, which is doubtful. No skiing and camping out by yourself in that world."

Alex was convinced they were both very good liars, and he never took his eyes off his hostess. Even when he looked out the window or went to the stove for another helping, he saw her in his peripheral vision or as a reflection in the window glass. He knew he was dancing with death, and in a strange way, he enjoyed it.

After dinner, Kate offered him coffee with some small cakes, then continued, "Tell me, how can you be comfortable living in a tent? You're of course welcome to stay overnight in the room you used to shower."

Alex accepted with a slight bow. He saw an opportunity.

"It's hard not to accept that invitation. To leave this warm and cozy house and go out to a cold and dark tent takes more willpower than I have. Thank you so much. But regarding sleep, I have always slept well out in nature. Maybe it's because of all the physical activities during the day, or maybe because of the silence. The only sound might be the wind or some animal. To me, the sound of nature is soothing. When I get back home, I always have sleep problems for a few nights."

"Interesting. So, you might lie awake tonight, tossing and turning?" Kate commented with a little worried expression. "If that's the case, I have some sleep aid I occasionally use myself. They work fine and leave no drowsiness the next day. I recommend them."

"I'm not a fan of pills of any kind. Any chemicals you put in your system to help it work better are actually depressing the body's own remedies. At least, that's my thinking. On the other hand, you learn by trying. What kind of sleep aid is it?"

"I'll get it for you. More coffee?" She got up from the table, grabbed the coffee pot, and refilled both cups. Then she disappeared into her bedroom. It took a couple of minutes for her to come back. Alex had no problem guessing why.

She showed him the bottle and let him read the label. *Take one to two tablets, as needed.* He took out two pills and held them in his hand. He thanked her and told her he would take them when he was in bed. He didn't want to get drowsy just yet. It was still way too early. If she was disappointed, she didn't show it. On the contrary, she seemed relaxed; she became more talkative and smiled more. Maybe in her mind, her mission was accomplished.

They continued their conversation, covering many topics. *When was the B&B's summer opening and closing? Did they have families?* She did not; he did. They talked about his wife, who'd been deceased for eight years, and his children and grandchildren. It was bizarre, at least for Alex.

At ten, Alex looked at the kitchen clock. He seemed surprised.

"My goodness, time flies in your charming company! It's time for me to call it a day. I plan to be up at six and on my way before seven. I really appreciate your hospitality and wonderful dinner, and I'd like to pay your normal charge for both the room and dinner. After all, you're running a business here."

"You're not paying anything," Kate said. "First, this place is not open for business yet, and second, I've had a great time myself. This has been an unexpected break in a boring routine of getting the place ready."

"I'll come back in the summer and stay a few nights. Now I know which room to ask for. Thank you so much. I'll go up and take the pills and hopefully sleep through the night."

"I'm sure you will sleep well. Good night, Alex."

Alex went up to his room and put on a T-shirt and sweatpants; his winter camping PJs were too warm in the house. He brushed his teeth and flushed the pills down the toilet, ignoring the thought of keeping one for analysis. He then tucked himself in, suspecting Kate would check on him in an hour or two. To her, he would appear deep in sleep, but he would be completely alert in case his killers showed up earlier than planned.

He listened to her clean up in the kitchen before making another telephone call, the words of which he could not hear. It didn't matter; the hunt was on. Now, he needed to breathe long and deep to slow his metabolism and make his body sound and feel like deep sleep. Occasionally, he peeked at his watch.

After about two hours, he felt her in the room. He hadn't heard any sound on the stairs or from the door; the house was very well-built. She was standing by the bed for a little while, listening to him breathe. Then she suddenly said in a loud voice, "Alex." She shook him, first gently, then with force. He waited for a needle to be pushed into his body somewhere. Nothing happened. She walked to the door and shut it with a loud bang, most likely still standing there, watching him. After a few seconds, she opened the door and left the room in a normal way. He could hear her movements.

It was past midnight. Alex was pretty sure his killers would show up well before four o'clock. Human nature; urgency takes priority. He listened for any activity in the house, but all was quiet. He slowly slid out of the bed and pulled the loaded gun from under the mattress. He took four extra cartridges and put them in his pockets. Then he moved into the adjacent room, facing the road just as quietly as Kate had moved. He put the gun on the bed and looked out the window. Here he would stand till the enemy showed, occasionally doing some stretching to stay alert in both body and mind.

The car arrived just after 1:30 a.m. The lights were very strong on the bigger road, probably due to extra halogen bars.

When the car turned onto the small road leading up to the house, all the lights except the parking lights were turned off. They parked next to Kate's pickup. Two men got out, both carrying guns, and walked toward the entrance.

Alex moved back into the room, grabbed his shotgun, and opened the door about four inches. They could not see the door from downstairs. He positioned himself on the floor with the barrel just inside the opening. He could barely hear a hushed discussion about the layout of the room and his position in the bed. Then they started up the stairs.

Alex saw them about halfway up: The first guy carried a gun; Kate was unarmed; the second guy also had a gun. None wore protective gear. He shot the first guy when he reached the third step from the top before shooting the second guy, both in the chest. Kate was too shocked to even scream. She just stood there for a couple of seconds. Then she tried to get the gun from the first guy who had rolled down to her feet. Alex reloaded his gun and shot her long before she had time to even get the guy's gun out of his hand. All three were dead within fifteen seconds and without any suffering.

Alex got up from the floor and looked down at the heap of bodies, or rather killers, lying on the stairs. Just like his reaction at the ski hut, he felt no guilt or regret. In his mind, people who steal defenseless children have given up their right to live. It was not a very complicated process to reach that decision.

Continuing to ski was out of the question. No new snow was in the forecast. Any visitor that came around could follow his tracks; he would be a sitting target within hours. He went back to his bedroom and got dressed in jeans, a pair of boots, a flannel shirt, a sweater, and a jacket. He rolled all his bedding and towels into a ball and threw them down to the kitchen area. His ski clothing went the same way. He then packed his backpack and dropped it down as well.

When he was done, he looked down at the mess on the stairs. The blood was now starting to cover the hallway. He climbed over the railing and succeeded in jumping off the stairs without getting into the bloody area.

In the kitchen, he found some large garbage bags and a toolbox. There was also a leather bag on the counter that he hadn't seen before. He opened it. It was filled with dollar bills packed in neat bundles as if they came straight from the bank. He stared at the money for a few seconds and then decided to take about half. If any uncompromised law enforcement agency examined the place, the money he left might give them a lead.

The bedding and towels fit into a large garbage bag, and his ski gear into another. With some effort, he got all of it out of the house without stepping in blood, which now covered most of the hallway. He walked to the gray pickup truck and threw it all in the back together with his skis, poles, and pulk.

The keys were in the ignition, as expected. With the tools, he removed the railing on the truck, which probably every cop in the county was familiar with. It took him a good half hour. When all was done, he went back into the house and turned off all the lights. The wall clock said 2:42.

It took him about fifteen minutes to get to the interstate. Traffic was light, and the road was clear of snow. He turned west and settled in at about seventy miles per hour. And now what? He had just killed three people, plus two at the hut and one in the Denver area. And at this very moment, he was driving a stolen truck belonging to a criminal in cohort with an unknown number of dirty cops. With the least little reason for somebody to stop him, he was a dead man. What the hell was he doing?

He turned down the guilt music and started to think constructively. First, he needed to get rid of the truck. It would still be nighttime for more than two hours. That would be enough to get to Eagle but not to Glenwood Springs. The Eagle airport's car park had to be his next stop. But even before that, he would have to dump all the garbage bags, skis, pulk, and ski gear.

The skis, poles, and pulk could have blown off a roof rack, so he started to look for a turnoff where he could get out and dump those items close to the road. That happened rather quickly when he came upon a salt and sand barn for the interstate maintenance.

His next dump, clothing and bed stuff, would be more delicate. He decided to put it all outside a Goodwill depot. He used his phone to Google a location. The next depot was in Eagle.

It worked as planned, and in good time before daybreak, he parked the car at Eagle Airport. He got his backpack with his tent and sleeping pad tied on the outside and started to walk toward the nearby river. It was a cool and dry morning, which promised a clear, sunny, and pleasant day. But right now, he felt totally exhausted. He soon found a spot not visible from the road and rolled out his pad and sleeping bag on top of a few inches of snow—no tent needed. He wiped off his boots and crawled into the sleeping bag fully dressed. Once inside, he fell into a restful sleep within seconds.

Chapter 4

Alex woke up from a bang. He tried to jump up, totally disoriented, and found himself tied down and in the dark. He couldn't stand up. It took some long seconds to realize he was inside his sleeping bag. With a sigh of relief, he unzipped the bag and looked out. The bang had come from a jet at the next-door airport that had just taken off. Its thunderous thrust knocked him out of his dreamless sleep.

It was almost nine o'clock on a cool and sunny morning. He had slept five hours and felt rested and alert. Still, he had no plan for the day, so he lay back down to ponder his next move. It wasn't very difficult. The supermarket a few minutes away with a gas station next to it would be job one: bathroom, food, and coffee—all he needed to get started. *Life is good*, he would have thought under different circumstances.

He stood up, arranged his clothes, and repacked his backpack. He found his wallet deep down inside it, checked its contents, and put it in his back pocket. The walk to the supermarket took about twenty minutes. He walked slowly, being in no rush—he actually enjoyed the morning sun and the normality of the early hours in a small American town. A place he could live in.

As the front of the supermarket came into view, he spotted two benches on one side of the entrance, baking in the sun. That would be a nice spot for some minutes of peaceful thinking.

But there were people sitting on both benches, three on one and two on the other. Well, he was not alone in his thinking. Better luck next time. Then, one of the twosomes stood up and walked toward the entrance. Alex caught himself speeding up, afraid that somebody else would suddenly show up and grab what had become his spot.

Not until he was seated did he pay attention to the other person on the bench: a woman, maybe in her forties, average size from what he could see, with dark blonde hair, a knitted cap, and an attractive profile. But what caught his attention was her very sad demeanor. She had no sunglasses, and her eyes were staring straight out in space, focused on nothing. He doubted she had even noticed his presence.

"Good morning," he said without looking at her, as he bent forward and started to dig around in his backpack. She said nothing. She probably didn't even hear him.

He got a bottle of water and a bag of trail mix and put them on the bench. He sat back, opened the trail mix bag, grabbed a handful of nuts and fruit, and started to eat. Then he turned toward the woman, pushed the bag and water bottle in her direction, and said in a fairly loud voice to make sure he got through her barrier, "Here, help yourself and drink some water. That could help clear your mind. I'm not a doctor of any kind, but with two kids and four grandchildren, I can see when somebody has a problem and needs a hand."

The intentionally long and loud sentence got her attention, and she turned her head in his direction. With a smile on her face, she would have been an attractive woman, but that was something for another time and place.

"Thank you," she said in a very soft voice and with an accent. To Alex's surprise, she reached out and took the water bottle. She opened it and drank half of it in one long gulp. She was dehydrated.

"I think you need some of these as well," he said and pushed the trail mix closer. "You have an accent. May I ask where you're from?"

Again, she turned her head and now actually looked at him. She was quiet for a while, as if she was deciding whether she should share anything with this stranger. She must have decided it was worth the risk.

"I'm from Russia," she said, then remained quiet.

"Oh, I've been to Russia. A few times. Moscow, St. Petersburg, Vladivostok. It's indeed a very large country. What part are you from?"

"St. Petersburg," she said, going again quiet for a few moments. Then she spoke again. "Why are you so kind to me? You don't know me."

Alex thought for a moment before he answered. "I guess I'm old-fashioned. If somebody is splashing around in the water calling for help, I jump in. I just couldn't take out my iPhone and take a video for my YouTube friends."

For the first time, Alex saw the shadow of a smile on the woman's face.

"What did you do in Vladivostok?" she asked. "The people I know who have been there took a train ride to see the country."

"No, it was business. I worked for the US State Department in those days, so there was no time for sightseeing. By the way, my name is Alex. I'm just passing through here."

"My name is Alina. Thank you for the water."

Then silence, and again she turned her head and stared out into nothing. Alex was silent for a little while. Then he spoke again.

"Alina, I don't know what's bothering you, but you look very troubled. I don't know if I can help you in any way, but please let me know if there is anything I can do, even a little bit. Do you need to call somebody? Do you need to see a doctor? Do you need food, transportation, anything?"

Then he waited for quite a while. At least she didn't immediately say no, which Alex took as a sign that she needed time to formulate what she should say. She started to talk in a very low voice, still staring straight out.

"I came here five months ago to visit my cousin. She had been here for a couple of years and had a good job. If I came, she knew I could get a job as well. It worked out as she had promised. I got a job doing simple stuff in an office. It was well-paid, and I had time to ski.

"After a few weeks, I got to know more about my cousin. She used some drugs and insisted I should try them. They were free, provided by the company. I didn't like that. I also felt that the company started to punish me for not using drugs. My time to ski was reduced and then eliminated. I knew I had to get away from there. I didn't know what their business really was, but there was always money and drugs around. I saved some money to get away and drive to Vancouver. I have a relative there, my father's brother, and I knew he could help me.

"But it was impossible to leave. There were two men at the place where I worked and stayed. One of them was always there to check on us—me, my cousin, and a couple of other girls. Then, late last night, or maybe early this morning, both those guys drove away. I took my handbag with my money and a duffel bag with some clothes, went out to the car they let me use, and drove away. I got here and stopped for gas. I took my bag to go in and pay. When I opened it, all my money was gone. My cousin didn't need any money. I think the two guys who were watching me took the money to stop me from leaving. They knew I wasn't happy. Now I cannot go back, and I cannot go home, or to Vancouver."

She stopped, seemingly exhausted, still staring out in front. It took only a moment for Alex to develop a plan for how to get out of enemy territory.

"Here are my thoughts. You want to go to Vancouver; I'm going to Seattle. You have a car; I have money. I'll give you money for gas right now, then I'm going in here and buy some fruit and snacks while you get gas. If you trust me, you come back here in front and pick me up. Saves me the flight ticket. If you don't trust me, you just leave and drive to Vancouver. But remember, you need a passport to get to Canada."

While Alex was talking, he dug into his backpack, took out a stash of twenty-dollar bills, and put them in the open trail mix bag. Being partially shielded by the backpack, he pushed the bag toward Alina. No need to be seen handing over a wad of money to a woman half his age sitting on a park bench. Not even at ten in the morning in a small mountain town.

Then he stood up, stretched his back, neck, and legs, grabbed his backpack, wished her a good day, and walked toward the entrance. Alina was too surprised to say a word.

After finishing his business in the supermarket, which took more than half an hour with cleaning up, brushing his teeth, and finding the items he needed, Alex walked outside. He gave himself a fifty-fifty chance she would be waiting. That way, he wouldn't be overly disappointed if she had left without him. After all, she didn't know him at all. When he scanned the parking area and finally saw a waving arm a few rows away, he was relieved. He would soon be out of here.

She drove as they left the area and headed toward the interstate. Alex suggested they stop for an early lunch before getting on the road. There were several restaurants to choose from around the intersection.

As they were ordering and eating, there was a noticeable change in Alina's mental balance. She was obviously smart. Without any planning, their talk was all about the weather and traffic, nothing important. They looked like an ordinary couple, a father and daughter, a husband and trophy wife. People could think what they wanted. But they did *not* look like two people who met an hour earlier and were both running for their lives. Which Alina didn't know either. Not yet.

As they left the restaurant, Alina walked with her arm under Alex's, like any normal couple. It was her own decision. Again, she got into the driver's seat, and Alex was glad she did. He still felt too shaken from everything that happened early this morning to be a safe driver on a busy road. He needed a few hours to settle down.

As they got onto the interstate, Alex began by asking a question that had nagged him for a while.

"What kind of vehicle did the two men drive when they left this morning? It could be good to know in case we meet them."

Alina suddenly looked worried again. She had not thought about that.

"It was a Ford pickup. Black with a lot of extra lights in front. I think it had F-350 marked on the sides. It was just a couple of months old."

Alex was silent. What were the chances? And when was a good time to tell her that he had killed the two men who stole her money? He only muttered, "Good to know."

They drove in silence for a few minutes. After a while, Alina started to talk.

"If they see us, they'll come after us. This is the road they often drive. The big boss lives down the road here. I'm worried. Maybe we should take a smaller road?"

"I wouldn't worry too much about that. This Tacoma is a very common pickup. And they would have to have eagle eyes to spot you inside going the opposite direction, and me being in the car should confuse them. Tell me about the big boss—what he looks like and where he lives."

"Well, he's about fifty. Unmarried, I think, but there are some women around. I was brought there a couple of times after I arrived. I had a feeling he was checking me out. We talked a bit. He said he was glad I had joined his company and that I had a bright future there. This must have been about four months ago. I haven't seen him since then. His house is coming up. It's right on the other side of the river. There's a bridge across the river to get there. It's a compound with several buildings and a few people living in it."

Alex sighed, then after a moment, he said, "Could you turn off at this upcoming rest area? I need to use the restroom. Too much coffee this morning."

Alina did what she was asked, and they both used the restrooms.

When they got back in the car and were ready to leave, Alex said, "I need to tell you something important, and please don't get upset or angry. This whole thing is totally shocking to me." He took a pause. Alina looked at him with a very worried face.

"I have been out skiing for over a week, camping out, relaxing, and enjoying nature and solitude," he continued. "I do that almost every winter. It started after I lost my wife eight years ago. But this time it was to get away after an attempt to kidnap my five-year-old grandson.

"I was visiting one of my daughters outside Denver and had taken my grandson to a playground. There were some loud cracks that sounded like gunshots. People panicked and ran. I looked for my grandson and saw him under the arm of a man walking toward a car. I ran after them and hit the man so hard he died. In the car was a female cop. I got my grandson home to my daughter without anybody recognizing us in the turmoil. I decided to take some time out to let things settle down and maybe hear some explanation about the cop in the car. That's why I took time out to ski the mountains.

"Yesterday afternoon, I came upon a small road with car tracks, so I looked down the road. I saw a large B&B among the trees and a woman walking toward me. She told me the place was closed for the season. But then she walked closer and really looked at me, like she thought she knew me but couldn't remember from where. She started to act very friendly. Then she invited me for dinner. For some reason, my instincts told me to accept.

"Inside the house, she said I could take a shower. I turned on the water and opened the door to the landing to try and find out what was going on. She was on the phone. She talked in a hushed voice, but I could hear what she said—that I might be the guy they were looking for. I met the description of the man who killed that kidnapper twelve days ago. The man she called, and another guy, came to kill me. They drove a big black Ford F-350, quite new and with a lot of halogen lamps in front. I killed them all. It was them or me."

He stopped and waited for her reaction. Nothing. After a few seconds of silence and her eyes looking straight ahead, like they had that morning on the bench, she turned toward Alex and looked at him.

"Thank you," she said in a soft voice.

Alex was taken aback. This must be a Russian reaction, or maybe just an Alina reaction. It was definitely not an American reaction.

They sat silent for a few moments. Alina again stared out the window. Then she spoke.

"You know, when you started to talk to me this morning, I sensed there was something different about you. That you cared. Now I know. I feel very safe, for the first time in many years." She looked at Alex with a smile and started the car.

They got back on the interstate and continued their travel. Nobody spoke for several minutes. There was a lot to digest.

After maybe ten minutes, Alina spoke again.

"We are approaching the area where the big boss lives."

"Could you slow down? And if there is an exit close by, I'd like to take a look at the place," Alex said.

Alina glanced over at him but said nothing. They arrived at an exit ramp. She drove down and stopped the car just before they got to the underpass.

"If we go any further, they can see us from the house. You can go closer and not be seen if you stay high under the bridge. I'll move the car a bit down this road to the right. Here is not a good place to park."

Alex got out and started to dig around his backpack. He got his binoculars, his sleep pad, and his shotgun pouch—just in case. He climbed up the ramp and walked across under the interstate to the other side. The walk was not comfortable, with about four feet of clearance under the interstate. When he reached the other side, he had a clear view of an impressive white mansion, a few other buildings, and a bridge across the river. A couple of cars were parked in the open area between the buildings, and three men were moving around on the well-cut lawn.

He rolled out his sleep pad, put down his binoculars, and opened the pouch. A disassembled gun in a pouch is not of much use. When the gun was assembled and loaded, he picked up his binoculars again. The bridge was about two hundred feet away and the buildings were over five hundred feet away.

Nothing noteworthy was going on. The guys were kicking a soccer ball, talking, and smoking. They were just hanging out, killing time.

Alex tried to decide what to do. He was lying under a bridge, looking at sunny, peaceful, and beautiful scenery—the headquarters of a very dark business. He thought the big boss was inside the building based on the presence of three bodyguards and a very impressive, president-style black Cadillac SUV.

Judging by the tranquility, they had no idea what happened at the B&B. But Alex knew that at some point, somebody would call and ask about the two guys who were some kind of bosses at the place where Alina had stayed—or been a prisoner. He decided to wait. It couldn't be more than a few hours, and the stakes were too high to just drive away. Alina would understand.

After a little over an hour, the front door of the main building opened, and a man came out. He moved fast, was well-dressed, and got the attention of the three men. He was a good-looking guy around fifty. The big boss! He walked over to the large SUV and got in the back. Two of the men got in the front. The black car was obviously hot from the sun. They started their journey by lowering the windows. The third man watched them as the car moved at low speed over the dirt road and across the narrow bridge.

Just before they turned right, away from Alex and onto the interstate ramp, they slowed down even more. That's when the first shot hit the man in the back seat through the open rear window. The second shot got the driver through the open front window. The car made a big jump forward, hit the interstate ramp, and tipped over. Alex reloaded. The man left behind on the lawn was first motionless for a couple of seconds. Then he pulled a handgun out of his belt. It was of no use at this distance. Alex's shot hit him, and he fell. It was probably not lethal, but he was out of commission. Alex finally took a shot at the underside of the tipped-over SUV, directly at the gas tank. It exploded.

He ran back toward Alina, who had heard everything and seen nothing. She had started the car and driven back toward the underpass when she heard the shots. She was visibly upset, very worried that something had happened to Alex. When she saw him running without even a limp, she smiled.

Alex threw the shotgun, binoculars, and sleep pad in the back and told her, "Just drive back onto the interstate and go westward."

Traffic on the interstate in both directions had come to a standstill, with people seeing the flames and smoke from the burning car. Some were trying to figure out if they could be of any help, but most were taking videos and selfies of the disaster for their YouTube friends. Hopefully, nobody paid attention to the gray Toyota Tacoma as it entered the interstate several hundred feet west of the fire.

Alina kept driving in a very controlled way, at the speed limit, while Alex disassembled and packed his shotgun. Not a word was said. Nothing needed to be said. They both had the same thought: The big boss of this crime organization was out.

Chapter 5

"Try to catch up with that car cluster ahead," Alex suggested as they were driving through the long and winding Glenwood Canyon. Alina increased the speed by a few miles per hour. A lone vehicle could make somebody take notice.

They kept driving in silence for several minutes. Alex broke it: "We have some decisions to make. Our first destination is Seattle. There, you can easily travel to Canada and Vancouver. I take it you have your passport."

After a few moments, Alina answered, "They took it with the money."

Again, silence for about a minute or two, until the peace was disrupted by several first responder vehicles: ambulances, police cars, and fire engines. A long caravan of piercing emergency horns ricocheted between the canyon's granite walls, a chilling reminder of the forces Alex had sat in motion.

The entire US law enforcement apparatus was now alerted to find out who had caused this fire, which had killed three people, and also shot a man found lying on the lawn, who was either wounded or killed. In a short time, they would find out that the guy on the lawn was the victim of a shotgun. And in the near future, that picture would also include three killings at a B&B, also by a shotgun—with same size pellets.

Alex and Alina exited the canyon and traveled along the interstate as one of many vehicles heading west. When they got through the crowded area around Glenwood Springs, Alex started to talk.

"Our destination is Seattle. The best way to get there is Interstate 84. That runs from Salt Lake City west to Portland, Oregon. I think we're better off staying on interstates with lots of traffic, at least till they start and look for this car. We should be OK today and through the night. Starting tomorrow morning, we'll monitor the news day and night.

"Now, this is how I see our situation. You are innocent of any wrongdoing. If we get questioned by law enforcement, you just tell the truth exactly how you told it to me. Every word of it, including how we met, where, and why.

"My situation is not so easy, but not hopeless. My name is unknown to law enforcement. I have no record, not even a speeding or parking ticket. On the contrary, if they check me up, they'll find that I've had security clearances to work at the State Department, military, and other government institutions around the world.

"Three years ago, I sold the business and retired. I was at the end of a several-day ski and hike outing, which are some of my hobbies, when I ran into you. From there, my story is the same as yours. The only thing that can nail me is the gun and the ammo. As soon as we hear that they're looking for this car, and for you, we have to dump both the car and the gun. Till then, I'll keep it. We may still need it."

Alina listened and said nothing. After a while, Alex continued.

"Alina, you didn't sleep at all last night. Let me drive so you can take a nap, maybe in the back seat. Just turn off at the next intersection."

"Thank you. I start to feel a little bit too sleepy to be a safe driver," Alina said as she glanced at Alex. "And you, are you OK after everything you've been through?"

"I feel very awake. Must be the adrenaline still pumping. And I've had more than an hour to relax, so I feel good. By the way, you've been in the US for about six months, and your English is flawless. Your accent is the only thing that gives you away. Did you study English in school back home? And what did you do before you came here?"

A lot of questions. Alina started to answer them.

"My parents were both teachers at a high school in St. Petersburg. It was kind of given that I should be a teacher as well, like my parents and my brother. My brother liked math, so he became a math and physics teacher. I liked math as well, but I was really more interested in history. In Russian schools, history teaching is all about the great Russia: its many victorious wars, the many bad tsars, and the many good leaders of the revolution and the People's Party. I did not embrace that as true history, and it only dealt with the last hundred years.

"So, I started to travel around Europe during our summer holidays to learn more—Greece, Italy, France, England, and, of course, our neighboring countries: Lithuania, Latvia, Estonia, Finland, Sweden, and Norway. The only common language I could use was English, which we had in school as voluntary courses. And I was married for about ten years. My husband, also a teacher, got into drinking. We have no children, so we separated a couple of years ago. That is one reason I decided to come over here, to maybe find a job as a teacher or translator. A new start."

Alina glanced over at Alex, who had been looking at her while she spoke.

"That explains a lot. Thank you. I'm sorry about the new start you got here. Maybe one day you can write a book about the adventurous year you spent in the US. But here comes a rest area. Turn off and let me take the wheel for a few hours."

After they switched and got back on the road, Alina soon fell asleep in the back seat. Alex drove and turned on the radio at a low volume that barely let him hear the news.

The local news was all about the fire by the interstate. A car had exploded, and everybody inside was dead. A man who had been shot was found in front of a house. He was seriously wounded and was now undergoing surgery at a hospital in Vail. Inside the house were three women and a man. They had heard several shots but not seen anything. They all lived there and were shocked by this horrible event. The man, by whom they were employed, was inside the burning car and presumed dead. But why? Nobody had an answer.

Several sheriff's deputies and police investigators were now at the scene, looking for answers to what had happened and why. At this point, they had no witnesses and no clues.

Alex was thinking. He had to ask Alina when she woke up if she had ever seen any young children pass through the place where she lived and worked or if her cousin had talked about children. He also had to ask her more about those drugs she talked about—what kind of drugs they were, where they came from, whatever she might have seen or heard around the place.

Then he started to think about the news he had heard five or six days ago—which seemed more like a month now. The FBI was involved because kidnappings had happened in several states. He tried to remember the agent who was interviewed. A lady. But what was her name? They could, of course, find her by calling the Denver FBI office. Alex decided not to worry about that and instead tried to figure out why he was so certain that all these people were involved in child trafficking.

The evidence chain wasn't very complicated. Those men had come to the B&B to kill him because he might be the guy who had upset the kidnapping in Denver and probably also killed the two deputies. There was, of course, a possibility that the two guys who came to the house were two different guys than those who left Alina's place. But he quickly dismissed that thought. It only meant there had been four bad guys out there instead of two.

He smiled to himself. If Alina had checked her bag and found out that the money was gone before she left, she would still be back there and not sleeping in the back seat of the car he was driving. Life certainly is a big lottery. The question right now for Alex was whether he had won or lost. Only time would tell.

Suddenly, he remembered the FBI agent's name. Linda, Linda Crawford—that was her name. He had a feeling he would contact her in the near future.

An hour later, Alex and Alina crossed the Utah border. Alina was still sleeping, and the longer, the better. He had decided he had a couple of other questions to ask her when she woke up: one about the B&B, and the other about her uncle in Vancouver. She had not called him "uncle." Maybe she was not familiar with that word.

They were now driving through the desert. No people, no cell towers, no news. The radio was turned off, and Alex's only company was his thoughts. He thought about Mike. He wondered if the chloroform had been strong enough to erase any memories of the kidnapping. He hoped so, not only for Mike's psychological balance but also for his safety. A young kid could easily drop a word that could be picked up by a teacher, who could then contact a psychologist, who could then contact the police. The road to hell is paved with good intentions. He forced that thinking away and found himself missing his family for the first time in twelve days.

He then reflected on the last eighteen hours, from the time he overheard the telephone conversation around ten o'clock last night, up till now, and all that had transpired in between. How unwavering he had been at the ski hut, the B&B, and then at the house when shooting those people. Was that normal? Would he wake up one day with some kind of PTSD? He had not hesitated at all, and he found himself without any guilt or regret.

It surprised him a lot, and it also made him realize that whatever the legal judgment would be in the end, he would never be considered a normal person. Not even by his family. The only conclusion was to keep his role in this mess a secret. At this point, only Alina knew about the day's shootings. It had to stay that way, if at all possible.

He had decided to stay on Interstate 70 until it intersected with Interstate 15, then take that north past Salt Lake City. An hour or so past Salt Lake they would get to Interstate 84. But now, they needed both gas and food. At the next truck stop, he slowed down and turned off. He drove slowly to a parking spot a little bit away from the crowded area.

Alina woke up before he stopped. The even humming of the road had kept her in a deep sleep. Her first reaction was some words he could not understand.

Alex said in a friendly voice, "Good morning, how was your sleep?"

Alina quickly found her bearings. "Good morning. How long have I slept?

"Three hours, give or take. Sorry to wake you, but we need gas, and we should eat," Alex said. "We're close to Salina, Utah, now. There's a shortcut to Interstate 15 that will save us an hour at least. After dinner, you can go back to sleep again."

"No, sir. Now it's your turn to sleep. I'd like to see some of this country now when I have the chance."

Alex was pleasantly surprised by her spunky response. He suggested they start by getting gas, then going to the restrooms and cleaning up before they had their dinner. It was almost five o'clock. He went in, paid in cash, and got gas. He was not using his credit card, for good reason.

After dinner, Alina took the wheel. Alex guided her to the smaller road through Salina and toward Interstate 15 North.

They drove on in silence until Alex suddenly noticed the time. It was almost six. He turned on the radio and dialed around until he found a news station. The top news was the car fire in Colorado. An SUV had exploded along the interstate, and three people were dead. The remnants were being examined for positive identification and cause of death, although three women and a man in a house nearby, from which the car had left, had told the police their names.

A man who had been shot and wounded outside that house was out of surgery and recovering. None of the four people in the house, or the wounded man, had any idea why the shooting had happened or who was behind it. None had seen anything. Not a trace had been found. All the victims worked for the same organization, a not-for-profit humanitarian group, doing much good work around the state. It was shocking!

Alina looked at Alex with something between fear and disgust in her eyes. After a while, Alex spoke.

"I'm not tired anymore. That was a real adrenaline kick. Maybe we should keep going. They haven't tied this car to the shootings yet, and the further we get, the better. We'll be in Idaho before we need gas again. Around ten o'clock. Then we can look for a room. What do you think?"

"I can sleep sitting here in the car, so I have no problem. But I must admit that the thought of a bed is kind of nice."

The traffic was light but would pick up as they got closer to Salt Lake City. They both were awake and alert. The desert they had been driving across had been brownish and grey with spots of green, but now they were again in a mountain area. The road and the lowland around it were bare, but the mountains were snow-covered and inviting.

"How is the skiing here, compared to Colorado? The mountains don't look as high here," she remarked.

"No, they are a bit lower by about a thousand feet or so, which is good for people who don't like the colder climate and lower oxygen level higher up. On the other hand, the ski season lasts longer in Colorado. Also, these are the mountains that catch the first snow as the moisture-loaded clouds blow in from the Pacific. The Utah mountains with their many ski resorts have the deepest and fluffiest powder anywhere."

Alina looked up at the mountains with a dreamy look in her eyes.

"What would you choose?" he asked her.

"Both! I'd come here and ski the powder, then go to Colorado for spring skiing," Alina said with a smile as she turned to look at Alex.

What could he say? Despite all that had happened over the last twenty hours or so, this woman seemed both smart and in control of herself. Alex decided to bring up another subject on his list.

"I like that plan. Something for next season: Another mountain that gets all its deep powder from the Pacific is Whistler, just outside Vancouver. But it's too close to the coast and not high enough for a long and reliable ski season. You can check it out when you get to your uncle. You called him your father's brother; we call that uncle. By the way, what's he doing in Vancouver? How long has he lived there?"

"Well, I don't think he's skiing," Alina started. "He's too old for that. And I don't mean his age but his condition. He's very heavy, like most Russians over forty. Too much alcohol and fatty food. And he works for the government. He's been a diplomat in different countries. He's been in Vancouver now for seven years, I think. He's over seventy years old and will probably retire after this job. He's the consul general at the Russian consulate in Vancouver. He is married, and his two sons live in Moscow."

"Very good. Now I understand what you meant when you said he could help you. His office can give you a new passport in a few hours. The only challenge is to get there. In Seattle, we can rent or buy a little sailboat and sail across to Vancouver Island. From there, you take a ferry to Vancouver and I sail back to Seattle. There is, of course, a possibility we get checked by the coast guard from both the US and Canada. But you have a true story to tell, which they can check, and your uncle can help as well."

Alina looked at him. "And what about you?" she asked.

"Don't worry about that. I'll tell them I took you there because I had a crush on you and thought I could talk you into staying. But it didn't work. Old men are fools around young girls, you know. They'll believe me," Alex finished.

Alina gave up a big belly laugh.

"That was brilliant!" she said when she could talk again. "Now I am certain that the book about my adventures in America will be a bestseller, and I will be rich and can retire and spend the rest of my life skiing the Utah powder. There are only two small problems with your plan: You are not an old man, and I am not a young girl. Besides that, it's fantastic!"

"Well, I didn't say it didn't need some polishing, but overall, I think it's pretty good. But I have another thing on my mind that we need to talk about. A very important thing. I want you to promise that all these killings today, which only you and I know about, will remain our secret as long as we live and wherever we live. Even if there were no legal consequences, I would be marked for life and viewed as some kind of lunatic. Even my own family would think I lost my mind and might disown me. I couldn't live with that."

Alina sat silent for several minutes. She finally spoke.

"I could promise you that, but I also have a request, and maybe we can make a deal." She looked at Alex with a bit of a twinkle in her eyes.

"What is it?" he asked. "If it's a lot of money, we have to take a detour to Las Vegas." He smiled at her, knowing after only hours together that it wasn't money she was after.

"No, we don't need to go to Las Vegas. And I don't think it would fit our schedule anyway. I still have a dream to come and live in the US, and even if I've seen the darkest side of this country during my stay so far, I believe I would be happier here than anywhere else. But I don't know a single person that I can talk to or ask for help or advice if I ever need it. I want you to promise that you, and maybe also your family, will be there for me and maybe let me visit sometimes. Like a cousin, if I ever get a visa to stay permanently when all this is over," Alina finished. She was very serious, and Alex felt it took a lot out of her to ask the question—or rather, the favor.

"We have a deal!" he said simply. Alina moved over and squeezed his arm, and that was it. They drove along in silent comfort.

As they approached the greater Salt Lake City area, traffic picked up. It was early evening, between rush hour and dinner hour. The road would be busy for the next couple of hours, until they had Ogden in their rearview mirror.

They listened to the news every hour. The headline news was the burning SUV in Colorado with three people dead. The fire had been hard to kill. The bodies inside were mostly charred, impossible to recognize and do any meaningful post-mortem on. The morticians would find some pellets if they were lucky. It didn't make much difference; they would be the same size they picked out of the wounded man on the lawn. More importantly, there were no answers to who was behind the shootings and why.

Alex and Alina found a hotel at a crossroads just over the Idaho border. It was past ten; they would get gas in the morning. Now they had only time and energy for two things: food and sleep. And with food, a glass of wine.

Alex had already explained to Alina that they would be safer sharing a hotel room and acting like a married couple. Nobody was looking for a couple at this point, and a man and a woman staying in separate rooms would more likely be noticed and remembered. Alina had no problem with that.

Alex went to the front desk. He asked for a room with two beds, which they had. He paid with his credit card, well aware that a credit card and a driver's license were required at every hotel and that nobody was looking for him at this point. He parked the car, and they both walked back to the hotel like a normal American couple.

They cleaned up and went to a restaurant next door. They got a table, sat down, and ordered their food and wine. Then they sat back and looked at each other face-to-face for the first time. They both smiled, and Alina said, "So *that's* what you look like. Not bad for an old man! Actually, you look younger face-to-face than from the side. Glad to meet you, Alex."

Alex looked at Alina and saw her eyes for the first time. They were the clearest blue eyes he had ever seen. She was a very beautiful woman. He was suddenly fully awake.

"Keep going. I suck up every word," he said. "And I had better check with my lawyer before I tell you what I see across the table. I don't want to get into any trouble."

Another belly laugh from this very intriguing lady. The few people in the restaurant turned and looked in their direction and smiled. *It's nice seeing older people in love*, they probably thought.

They got their wine and drank a toast to life. Then Alina toasted Alex; all that had happened was thanks to him. The food arrived and interrupted their little ceremony, to Alex's relief. Within the last twenty hours, he had killed six people and wounded one. A few days before that, he had killed three other people without even knowing if they all were bad. It would take a long time before he could feel anything like a hero, if ever.

They finished their meals, paid, and went back to the hotel. It was awkward for Alex to be in a bedroom with a woman other than his wife. But he had a plan. He said to Alina, "You take the bed closest to the bathroom. I'll take this one. I'll lie down and rest while you get ready."

Without waiting for her response, he lay down on one of the beds and closed his eyes. Alina smiled at his old-fashioned procedure. She got into the bathroom and got ready in less than ten minutes. When she got back out, she heard soft snoring from Alex's bed. He was totally out, and she was not going to disturb him. If he slept till noon the next day, it would be fine with her.

Chapter 6

For several days, Linda Crawford had been getting increasingly frustrated. It was Wednesday morning. She had worked ten days trying to trace the sender of the message regarding "a delivery" without any results. The sheriff in the county from which the message originated, Chuck Thompson, had interviewed all his deputies and staff and come up emptyhanded. Could the sheriff be involved as well?

Linda decided to drop that thought and accept the fact that the communication system Colorado law enforcement worked with did not require an ID to send a message. This person knew enough not to use his or her personal device. There were over forty people, including deputies and staff, who had access to twelve office computers.

At lunchtime, Linda knocked on Steve Callahan's door. He barked his normal "Enter!" Linda walked in.

"Steve, are you free for lunch? I'm so darn frustrated, and I need to vent."

"OK, Linda, just give me two minutes to get this email off."

Linda killed the minutes pacing the corridor, thinking of nothing and feeling miserable. She was suddenly slapped back to reality by a familiar sound. From somewhere in Colorado, a 911 call had come in, reporting both shootings and explosions. Even if the FBI had no immediate responsibility to respond, they were alerted when exceptional events happened. And this event was exceptional.

All agents in the office gathered in the conference room to get a picture of what was known at this point. It was both very little and a lot: A car had exploded with people inside. A man was shot and lying on the ground. It all happened at an entrance ramp to Interstate 70 in Eagle County. First responders were on their way.

Linda was suddenly out of any frustration. She, like everybody else, sat silent, waiting for their boss, Tom Baker, to give his comments and possibly instructions. It didn't take long.

"Good afternoon," Tom began. "At this point, we don't know if we'll get involved in this event, but it is likely we will. Eagle County is also where Linda and Steve have some unfinished business. And you all remember one of the first things you learned at the Academy: If you believe in coincidences, you don't belong in law enforcement. I instruct Linda and Steve, and two additional agents that Linda will select, to prepare for deployment. Get the jet on standby, and book cars and rooms in Eagle. Open-ended. That's all for now."

Linda got to work. She instructed one of the office administrators to take care of the jet first, then the cars, and finally the hotel. She then went over to Steve, who was expecting her.

"OK, I'm ready for lunch now," he joked, but immediately got back to business. "Let's hope this is the break we've been waiting for. Regarding the two guys, you go first."

"I have three names: Bob Jonson, Susan Winkler, and George Moore."

"I like all three. Just off the bat, I don't know whom to drop. We can ask them if anyone would rather stay back for any reason. If no one volunteers, we have a draw. Nobody will feel excluded that way."

Linda thought for a few moments. "I like that idea, and I'm ready to go with it. But I would like to run it by Tom. Not for his approval, but to hear if he has any thoughts regarding any of them, like another job or so. OK?"

Steve had no objection, so Linda walked over to Tom's office.

"Steve and I agree on three agents. I'm not asking for your opinion, only if any of them are on another assignment, so you would rather keep them here. Otherwise, we'll select two of them."

Linda gave Tom the three names. He walked slowly up to the window and looked out for a few moments. Then he turned around and looked at her.

"I've thought about this whole situation. A car exploding with people inside—how many, we don't know yet—and an additional man being shot is a highly unusual event. If the reality is even close to what it looks like, it can become difficult out there. You'll need six additional agents, and even if you don't ask for my opinion, I think the ones you mentioned are the best of the best for this job. And I'll call our Glenwood Springs office and have them send over three agents when you land.

"The other thing I thought of is to take the chopper instead of the jet. Time to and from airports eats up a big part of the speed difference, and you may need local transportation as well. Good luck, Linda."

Back in his office, Linda gave Steve the news and said she would ask the three agents to meet them in the conference room. In less than a minute, all five agents were gathered.

"Tom has concluded that we need eight agents on this job if we get involved: us five and three from Glenwood Springs. You're the ones Steve and I have selected," Linda opened. "First question: Does anyone have an issue with spending the next several days in Eagle?" Three heads shook no. "Good. I think we have a great team. Let me update you on the reason for the urgency here. You're probably aware of last Saturday's kidnapping incident. We have not been able to find either the man who ran after and saved a child or the child himself.

"That is unusual since the media have repeatedly announced that the man who killed the kidnapper is not facing any charges; he's only wanted for information. The most unusual part of this tragedy is that both the kidnapper and the driver are dead; the driver died by suicide in the holding cell in this building. The only trace we have is an email to the deceased policewoman from a computer at the sheriff's office in Eagle County. I believe all this is old news to you.

"What may not be well known is that there has been a string of kidnappings in the northwestern states over the last six months. I have been assigned to look into that for possible connections and clues. Our conclusion is that we are dealing with an international crime organization, likely based in Russia, doing not only kidnappings but also drug smuggling and human trafficking. Today we had a vehicle explosion and shootings in Eagle County. That's all we know at this point. Call your families and gather your vacation bags. Let's get together here in ten minutes. Thank you."

They were all sitting around the table at the ten-minute mark. Linda showed up a couple of minutes late.

"Tom just got off a call with Sheriff Chuck Thompson," she began. "There were three people in the car that exploded. The sheriff sounded overwhelmed and would welcome the FBI's involvement. It's not the usual reaction, so it's an indication that this will require resources that the sheriff's office just doesn't have.

"This investigation will be a challenge. We are dealing with an unprecedented act of violence toward a large private property seemingly with only one purpose—to kill the owner of that property and, in the process, his guards.

"I can think of only three motives: a gang war, a personal vendetta, or an act of vigilance. In either case, it would suggest that the owner of the property, Mr. Andrew Palinski, who is among the three who died in the explosion, had developed some very fierce enemies. What activity or activities was Mr. Palinski involved in that brought this kind of violence upon him? According to the media, he ran a not-for-profit organization. We can almost certainly conclude that this was a front. Mr. Palinski was involved in other things, and our job is to find out what they were.

"What should bother us is that the sheriff's office was the source of the email that led to the failed kidnapping attempt here. We cannot exclude anything, so our first priority when on-site will be to seal off all buildings. Everybody has to come outside.

"Then, my plan is to give each of you a group of officers to work with. Let me start with you, Susan. There were four people inside the main building when the shooting happened: three women and one man. At least, that's what's been reported. I'd like them all back here for interrogation and whatever treatment they might need.

"Tom has requested three additional agents from Glenwood Springs to meet us when we land. I want you to take one of them, then go find the four people and take them down here right away in the chopper. Go and prepare for their arrival now before we leave. After dropping them off here, you and the agent will fly back. And make sure there is no communication between the four suspects during transit."

Susan Winkler left the room to inform staff about the arrival of four "guests." The five agents all grabbed their equipment and private duffel bags before heading for the door and the waiting Bell-407 helicopter.

Well in the air, Linda proceeded with her plan. They would gather everybody in front of the main building or inside if there was an appropriate room. She would then introduce the five of them and explain how the work would proceed.

Over the intercom, she contacted the pilot with a question.

"Captain, do you have the ability to take air photos of the ground we fly across?"

"Yes, we do. Anything in particular?"

"I would like to have pictures of the property we are going to from high enough to detect any earth disturbances—excavations, grave diggings, and the like."

"Roger that. Maybe before landing, so you get the lay of the land as well."

"Perfect. Thanks, Captain!"

There were still fifteen minutes in the air left. Linda called her assistant.

"Karen, Linda here. Can you find out the status of the guy who is at Vail Hospital with shot wounds? Call me back ASAP. Thanks."

They traveled over some of the most spectacular sceneries anywhere—the highest parts of the Rocky Mountains, the Continental Divide, rivers, and lakes. And nobody had time or was in the mood to enjoy any of it.

Linda got a call back after a few minutes.

"The man has gotten eleven pellet wounds, none of them critical or very deep. He can be discharged any time," Karen reported.

"Very good. Now go right over to Tom and ask him to interfere so the man is kept at the hospital and in isolation as a critical witness until an FBI agent picks him up," Linda instructed.

Then she turned to Susan. "Susan, that guy who was shot and taken to the hospital is ready to be discharged. You should take him with you to Denver. Ask the pilot to pick up the guy at the hospital as you leave. It would save us a lot of time."

The pilot brought the helicopter in at high altitude over their landing spot. From there, he circled down slowly so that he covered the entire surroundings outside the group of buildings that made up the compound.

It was indeed a large estate. It contained a huge white main building, several red houses and barns over a few acres, and beyond, rolling fields and forests. There were no clear indications, like fences or ditches, where the property lines ran.

As they were down and waiting for the rotor to stop, the pilot called Linda.

"We have about five hundred pictures. They will be analyzed tonight and tomorrow. You should have an answer in a day or two."

"Thank you so much, Captain. That's more than I expected."

"It's part of our job. I understand you want us on standby?"

"Yes, and not for long. We hope to have some witnesses that should go back to Denver as soon as we find them, and that also includes a guy at Vail Hospital," Linda finished as she departed the helicopter.

The first one to meet them on the ground was Sheriff Chuck Thompson. Linda greeted him. "Good afternoon, Sheriff Thompson. My name is Linda Crawford, and I am the agent in charge. Do you have a place we can sit and review the situation here?"

"Yes, let's go to the main house. I think the dining room will be a good place, and it may work as a command center as well."

As they walked toward the large white mansion that dominated the sprawling compound, the sheriff reminded Linda about their telephone conversation ten days earlier about an email. It was quite a coincidence they would meet so soon after, for a very different and very tragic reason. Linda said nothing. The sheriff led her to the large dining room. She stopped for a moment and looked around. With a few rearrangements, it would be perfect as a command center. When they were seated, the sheriff spoke. "First, I want to thank you for the fast response. This unbelievable event is far too complex for our office to handle. We simply don't have the manpower or expertise. I appreciate that the FBI takes the lead in the investigation, and my deputies and I will give you all the support we are capable of."

"Thank you, Sheriff," Linda said. "Let me first express my condolences to you and the entire community for the tragedy that happened here today. I am aware that every single person who lives here is expecting answers as to who and why this crime was committed. I will not rest until we have those answers.

"I will not ask you personally to be part of this investigation. You have a more important job to do—to keep the county safe. But I would like a few extra eyes for our investigation groups, and then some of your deputies to take care of general security and traffic, keeping the public and the media out during the day and keeping this place safe during the night. Who would you suggest heading that group?"

"My most respected deputy is Matt Darby. He's been with us for close to thirty years and knows our procedures and people better than anybody. I planned to leave him here for that reason anyway."

"Thank you, Sheriff. I appreciate that. I'd also like for you to come around whenever it's convenient, partly to help us out and answer questions we might have and partly to be a liaison between us and the community."

The sheriff agreed and hoped for speedy progress in solving this incredible crime.

After the sheriff left, Linda walked out and met the three agents from the Glenwood Springs FBI office: Brian Thompson, Jeff Conner, and Roger Smith, all young and professional-looking men. She welcomed them and asked Brian and Jeff to summon all deputies and state troopers not tied up in traffic control to join them in ten minutes. She asked Roger to help her rearrange the dining room to work as a command center.

It didn't take long. Plates, glasses, vases, and silverware were moved into the kitchen. The dining table was moved a couple of feet to make room for a flip chart they had brought, and a few chairs were moved around. As they finished, people started to fill the room. There were somewhere around thirty bodies in all. Linda walked up to the flip chart at the short end and wrote her name.

"Good afternoon, ladies and gentlemen. I am Special Agent Linda Crawford. At the request of Sheriff Thompson, the FBI is now leading this investigation, and I am the agent in charge. Going forward, we will work in task groups headed by special agents and one traffic and security group, which I will ask Deputy Matt Darby to lead. When we are done here, I would like to have a word with Deputy Darby.

"At this point, I see four task groups. If possible, each should have representation from both the sheriff's office and the state troopers for the broadest expertise. Group one will be responsible for interrogating the four witnesses and the lone survivor. It will be led by Special Agent Susan Winkler. Susan is already on her way to locating these people. Group two will be responsible for fine combing the entire property for leads. It will be led by Special Agent Steve Callahan. Group three will be responsible for searching documents, computers, telephones, and the like. It will be led by Special Agent Bob Jonson. Group four will be responsible for searching for the firing site or sites for any traces left behind. It will be led by Special Agent George Moore. The three agents who are here will now pick their teams and go to work. Those who do not get picked, I'd like to talk to you."

When all was set in motion, Deputy Darby came up and introduced himself. He was a large, confident-looking man whom Linda immediately felt comfortable with. Linda suggested they sit down for a talk.

"First, Deputy, let's skip the frills. Call me Linda. I hope you're fine with me calling you Matt."

"Thank you, that's what the entire county calls me. I may not pick up on anything else."

"Good, thank you. I'm going to share my thoughts with you and then ask for your feedback. First, this is a very large estate, and we have a huge interest from both the media and the public. Even if we have the river as a buffer, we cannot rule out people finding some back roads here. Another thing we have to keep in mind is the nature of the crime. Judging from what happened and the violence of the attack, we must expect that Mr. Palinski did other things than what is publicly known. We cannot rule out that there are associates of Mr. Palinski who would try to come here and destroy evidence, computers, and documents. In summary, we need heavy traffic control during the day and heavy property security during the night. Your turn."

Matt was deep in thought for a while, and then he spoke. "You know, we've gotten so used to looking upon Mr. Palinski as a totally straight and honest person that the alternative never dawned on us. Now, after you mentioned it, I realize that he must have had some very serious enemies, however that had happened, and also some very close associates-in-crime, who now are concerned about being exposed. It's your job to find the enemies who shot him and the associates who may try to destroy records and other evidence, and it's my job to make sure the buildings remain intact here so it can be done. I'll talk to a couple of guys and put together a day program and a night program and present it to you in about an hour. Is that OK?"

"Thank you, Matt. That would be great."

With that, the big man headed out. Linda called Susan and asked if she had found the four witnesses.

"Yes, and we are all in the caretaker's apartment," Susan said. "There is one family of three: a husband and wife and their fifteen-year-old daughter. Their apartment is in one of the red buildings. They are Colombians with clear immigration statuses. They have been here for eleven years, and their English is good. Both parents work here, the wife cleaning and cooking and the husband taking care of the properties. He has keys to all the buildings.

"With them is also a seventeen-year-old au pair girl from Germany. Her bedroom is upstairs in the main house. She is the one who seems most traumatized by what happened here. There is another apartment next to the caretaker's apartment, with several bedrooms, which are used by different visitors, who came and stayed for a few days."

"Good, Susan. Can you ask the German girl to show you her bedroom before you leave? I'd like to see it too, so just bring them all over."

A couple of minutes later, Susan and the four witnesses came into the dining room. Linda and Susan followed the German girl upstairs to her bedroom. Linda asked her name, which was Hilde.

"Do you want to pack some of your personal things?" Linda asked. "Nobody knows when anybody can come back here."

Hilde could not come up with an answer. She was clearly distraught and would need medical attention.

Hilde's bedroom was down the hall from the master bedroom. There were five bedrooms in total, all with their own full bath. As an au pair, she really had luxurious accommodations.

Linda asked Susan if she thought the father was trustworthy. His knowledge could be an asset.

"Yes, I think he is. He seems very concerned about his family and their situation. He doesn't seem at the least aware of anything else going on. They work here and the girl goes to school. There are a lot of religious books and pictures in their apartment. They have a good life here and are afraid it will come to an end."

"OK, let me talk to him. We need someone who knows the place. It's a very large property."

Susan agreed. She told her group that the husband would stay behind to help out with all they had to do. The wife looked very upset when she heard that but said nothing.

After the changes, Susan, Jeff, the two Colombian women, and Hilde left for the helicopter. In a few minutes, they would be picking up the wounded man at Vail Hospital.

Linda asked the husband and the two remaining agents, Brian and Roger, to wait for her in the dining room. She walked over to the place where Steve Callahan was assembling his group. There were four officers, Steve, two deputies, and a state trooper. Steve gave his instructions.

"We will start in the main house and go from room to room. Gloves and shoe protection are always mandatory. All suspicious items shall be flagged and photographed but not touched. In due time, specialists will come and take care of our findings."

"Could you use another agent?" Linda asked.

"Yes, I could. And more than one, if possible."

"OK, I'll send over Brian Thompson. We are keeping the caretaker to help us out."

Linda went back to the dining room and took Jeff and Brian aside.

"I'll give you some background so you understand what's going on here. About ten days ago, we had a failed kidnapping attempt in Littleton, a Denver suburb. You probably know about that. In our investigation, we found an email sent from the sheriff's office here in Eagle to the female police officer who was involved in the attempt. She was instructed to expedite the delivery of an item no later than the following Monday. When asked, she refused to answer any questions and took her life in our custody. In spite of his efforts, Sheriff Thompson has not been able to pin down the sender, so we know that his organization is compromised. What we are doing by putting a deputy in every work group is to hopefully find a deputy on the wrong side. It's a long shot, but still a shot," Linda explained. "Brian, go over to Steve's group, and Roger, come with me."

Linda and Roger went back to the dining room–turned–command center. She introduced them both to the caretaker and asked him to tell his life story, the five-minute variant. The man looked uncomfortable as he tried to find the right words, but that soon passed.

"My name is José Delgado, and I am forty-five years old. I grew up in a small town called Neiva, south of Bogota in Colombia. My father owned a grocery store, and our lives were good. But that changed in the late 1990s when the FARC guerilla tore the country apart. Our grocery store was ransacked and destroyed, and our whole family—my parents, my older sister, and myself—fled south to Ecuador with nothing but some savings. There, we found work on the flower plantations around Quito. We cut flowers in the fields ten hours a day, flowers that would be displayed in supermarkets all over the US the next day. I never stopped thinking about a life in the US.

"After eight years in Ecuador, where we saved every penny, Maria—the woman I had met and married—and I could fly to the US. We came to Miami. The air was so thick, it was hard to breathe. A young immigration officer we talked to said we should go to Colorado, to the Rocky Mountains. He had visited Quito, so he understood our situation, coming from nine thousand feet to sea level. We went to Eagle County, Colorado. After a year, we got our green cards, and a year later, in 2009, our daughter Sofía was born.

"We made a living working different jobs, mostly cleaning, construction, and yard work—anything that paid the bills. In 2012, we were hired by the previous owner of this property. He was mostly traveling all over the world. Here we got an apartment, didn't have to travel to work, and got benefits. Everything we could dream of had come true.

"Four years ago, the owner decided to sell the house. We were afraid our happiness would all end, but the new owner offered to keep us and even gave us a raise. We were very happy. This is the only home Sofía knows, and she has made many friends, both in school and in church. All this may end now."

Linda sat silent for a long time. She couldn't help reflecting on life's ironies. In the middle of this unbelievable disaster, she had just listened to the most uplifting life story. She finally got back to reality.

"José, I am moved by your story, and I can promise you that if you help us solve this crime, your work records and our contacts will land you and María another job. Maybe not right here, but in Colorado, and all of you will be just fine. So, let's go to work.

"The attack on this property is extraordinary. This is a very unusual crime, to say the least. What it points to is the elimination of a competing crime organization—a gang war, in other words, well-planned and skillfully executed. This scenario can, of course, be totally wrong, but that's what it looks like. You have been here many years. Have you seen or heard anything over the years that looks strange or suspicious to you? Have you seen drugs, money bags, or delivery trucks passing through? Why were there so many guards around? What line of work was your employer in? I will let you think about what was going on here, and I'll be back in a few minutes."

Linda and Roger left the room and went to see how Steve Callahan and his team were doing. They found them in the owner's office, standing around doing nothing. The sheriff's deputy was sitting on a chair. Handcuffed.

Linda looked around for a couple of seconds, taking in the scenery. "I see you are making some kind of progress. Can you fill me in?"

"Yes," Steve said. "We made clear nothing could be touched, only recorded. This man had a problem with that. He was seen putting some plastic bags in his pockets. When confronted, he denied the accusation and refused to be patted down. When we approached to check him, he reached for his gun. Two of our guys took him down. He had pocketed five different packages, all containing substances. And that's where we are. We can hold him overnight in Glenwood and take him to Denver in the morning. A car to Denver now would run into stop-and-go traffic all the way. What do you think?"

"I think this is going very well. Get his phone and search his home and office for computers, pads, and other devices. Take him out of here and put him under a twenty-four-hour watch. However sad this is, it's a step forward in our investigation.

And all you guys, not a word about this for now. Maybe we can catch another one. And you need a replacement. Roger here is looking for something to do."

Linda left the room and headed back to José. As she entered the room, she immediately saw that José was uncomfortable. She took a seat opposite him.

"You are looking troubled, José. What's on your mind?"

The poor man, who she knew was forty-five years old but looked ten years older, moved around on his chair as if in pain. After a few moments, he started to talk, with difficulty.

"María and I like it here very much. But it has become difficult. The young girl, Hilde, who has been here almost a year, has become a friend of our daughter. María cleans the bedrooms in this building. She has told me that Hilde often sleeps with Mr. Palinski, and they also use drugs. Hilde has also tried to give drugs to Sofía. We are so worried."

"Well, José, one good thing about this disaster is that you will never have to worry about Hilde again. She will soon fly back to Germany. But as far as drugs are concerned, is there anything else you can think of that you have seen or heard? And why are there so many guys around, like bodyguards? Maybe you can show me the apartment they stay in?"

José looked relieved, both from Linda's response and from a chance to move around. Sitting in a chair and being interrogated was nothing he cared for. They left the main house and walked across a big lawn over to the nearest red building. There were two front doors, one to the caretaker's apartment and the other to the guest apartment. José led the way over to the second door.

Linda stopped before they entered and told José, "José, this entire property is a crime scene. Everything will be searched for leads. We cannot touch anything, only look, and we both must put on gloves and shoe protection." She took out a bag with the required items, and they both put them on.

They entered the apartment and walked through a small vestibule into the great room. It was a comfortable room, with a couch and four armchairs around a coffee table; a big TV on the wall; a small kitchenette with a cooktop, a microwave, a large refrigerator in one corner; and a small dining table next to it. The room had not been cleaned this morning, and the normal assortment of bottles, beer, whisky, sodas, as well as glasses, coffee cups, ashtrays, and snack boxes, littered the table—an all-American man cave.

Upstairs were four bedrooms, each with two single beds and a full bathroom. There were no signs of drugs or anything suspicious.

They left the apartment. Linda thanked José for his help and told him not to worry about his family. He would soon see them again.

It was almost six o'clock. Linda walked toward the bridge to see how George Moore and his team were doing. Halfway there, she met Matt Darby. He waved at her from some distance.

"Linda, do you have a minute?" He didn't wait for an answer. "I can have eight deputies and eight troopers divided into two groups, one for daytime and one for nighttime, each working twelve-hour shifts. The day shift would have six officers doing traffic and two on security; the night shift would have the reverse. Four of the day shift guys will sleep here as backup if we get visitors. What do you think?"

"I have given this some thought, and my biggest problem was the potential need for additional manpower if there is a problem during the night. You solved that. Go right ahead with your plan. Thanks, Matt."

Linda continued her walk across the bridge. She was relieved that one of the most important issues, the twenty-four-hour security at this sprawling compound, was in competent hands.

Across the bridge, she saw two of the officers crawling around just under the overpass, while George and another officer were examining the road about three hundred feet away. As Linda approached, George walked up toward her. He started his report.

"We found the shooter's spot up there." He pointed toward the two officers. "He had a protected place where he could have been waiting a long time for the right moment. It's amazing they had not closed that off. It's like they never thought anybody would come after them. The shooter was lying on a sleeping mat, quite comfortably, but more importantly, not leaving a single trace behind. The only things we have been able to find are gun smoke on several rocks and some threads from the mat. I bet a hundred bucks that there will be no DNA on those threads.

"The shooter must have had a car and a driver, and if he stayed around for some time, the car must have been parked somewhere else. As soon as he saw people walking toward their car, he summoned the driver. That's how we see this whole thing going down. Nothing left behind, like an instructor showing how to do it."

After a moment, Linda spoke. "What you are suggesting is that we are dealing with a shooter and a driver. An army of two. Not a gang war at all, but a vigilante. Maybe a member who got disgusted and turned on them."

George thought for a moment and then said, "I haven't gotten that far yet. I only told you what we found. There must have been four shots fired. With an ordinary shotgun, that means it had to be reloaded. No empty shells were left behind. We are dealing with a very cool shooter—a guy on a mission, a person who knows the area and the people. Part of the family, so to speak. I agree with what you already said: a vigilante."

"OK, George, if you guys are done here, why don't we all meet back in the dining room and talk some more? Let's say, in ten minutes."

With that, Linda started to walk back toward the main building. A tow truck had finally got the burnt-out wreck up on its deck and was ready to drive away. Linda crossed the bridge, and it struck her how beautiful the whole setting was: the river, the mountains, the green lawns surrounding the well-kept buildings. It was the perfect place to enjoy life.

Linda called Susan and asked for an update.

"Only good news here," Susan reported. "There were no surprises during the transport. All four are checked in at the hospital for evaluation. The man is anxious to get back. He is a sheriff's deputy who makes some extra money working security at Mr. Palinski's ranch. He doesn't have the foggiest idea why somebody would attack such a fine and generous man as Mr. Palinski. He calls him a pillar of the community."

"Thanks, Susan. I hope we soon find out what kind of pillar Mr. Palinski was. Here we had some serious action. A deputy working with Steve pocketed some dope, and when confronted, he went for the gun—in the middle of all these cops. I've never heard of anything like that before. He's in our custody in Glenwood. Can you check with the pilot if he can make another trip this evening with two extra agents to bring the guy back to Denver?"

"Will do. Bye for now." Susan ended the call and called back after a couple of minutes. "The pilot doesn't have enough airtime left to do the trip, but if it's urgent, he can call in another pilot."

Linda thought for a moment and decided against it. Susan and Jeff would return with the chopper the following morning, and it was highly unlikely that the deputy had been walking around with a cyanide pill on his body.

Linda contacted Steve and Bob and asked them and their teams to join her in the dining room in ten minutes. When they were seated, Linda began speaking.

"We have been here for about three hours. Not a very long time, but enough to determine that this place is clean, at least on the surface. The caretaker and his family have lived here for eleven years, taking care of everything. They are very religious, and they have worked extremely hard to get to this country and make a living here. When I asked the man if he had ever seen anything suspicious, illegal, or bad, he was utterly uncomfortable as he told me that his wife, who cleaned the houses, had told him that the owner slept with Hilde, the seventeen-year-old au pair from Germany. And they also used some drugs. His concern was how that might affect their daughter. That's it. This could just as well be a religious summer camp.

"The whole place is well-planned and tastefully built. It's a presentable estate where businesspeople and community leaders have met and socialized. And yet, an unbelievable mass murder happened here six hours ago! What I want us to focus on now is electronics. Communication. Bob, it's your area. Use us all to really look deep for any communication that can shed some light on the dark secrets of this place. That's all for now."

Linda called Tom Baker. He picked up immediately, obviously anxious to hear their progress. Linda had decided to cut all BS.

"Hi, Tom, the important finding here is that this is not the place we thought or hoped it was. The only illegal thing we found is the owner's affair with an underage German girl—underage here, but probably not in Germany. Otherwise, the place is clean. A successful man's impressive residence.

"We have gotten verification that the deputies here are dirty. How many, we don't know. I will talk to the sheriff about that as soon as we hang up. I suggest we stay another day and see if we can find any lead to whatever caused the murders. And how was your day, sir?"

"Just fine, thank you. And Linda, don't forget that the night is darkest just before first light. I wouldn't be surprised if tomorrow is a great deal different. Thanks for your update, and good luck on the hunt tomorrow."

Linda called Sheriff Thompson. He was in his office, waiting for her call. Rumors about the arrested deputy had reached him. He was naturally upset. Linda invited him over. They would have a private room to talk.

The sheriff arrived after about fifteen minutes. He looked both tired and old. They found two comfortable chairs in one of the living rooms.

"I'm sorry over the incident that forced us to arrest a deputy. What can you say that might shed some light on the matter?" Linda asked.

The sheriff started with a deep sigh. "This deputy, Ben Sanders, has been with the force for over ten years. He was a hardworking and reliable man. Like many of the younger guys, he looked for extra hours, particularly on weekends when the pay was better. After a couple of years, I realized he had money problems. From gambling, he said when I brought it up. I told him that he had to get control of that problem if he wanted to stay with us. He said he would. He said he loved his job. I thought he cleaned up his act, but maybe not. We never found out who sent that mail a couple of weeks ago. It has bothered me since we talked, and maybe we've found the answer now."

There was a long pause. Then Linda said, "I hope we find that person as well, but we can't jump to any conclusions. One possibility is that he just wanted to sell some dope and make some extra money. But of course, that doesn't explain him going for the gun. That's the serious part of this incident. Maybe we'll have an answer in a couple of days when we check his phone and computer.

"On a different subject, I would like to talk to you tomorrow, when it's convenient, and try to get some understanding of what may be behind all that happened here. I want to know what kind of person Frank Palinski was, as you knew him. It may help us, and it may not. Is that OK with you?"

The sheriff stood up. "I'm not sure I have anything of value to add, but I can come back tomorrow around this time and share what I know."

After reflecting on the conversation for another few moments, Linda went over to the home office to chat with Steve.

"Have you found anything of interest?" she asked.

"Yes, we found the safe. It's an ordinary type; our people should have no problem getting into it tomorrow. We also found something else, in the basement. You got a minute?"

The question was rhetorical. Steve was already heading toward the stairs. They again walked down to the huge game room, at least fifty by thirty feet. It had a sitting group in front of a fireplace and a huge TV at one end, with a wet bar to the side. There was a pool table in the middle and several different games at the other end where they had just come down.

"Look at this," Steve said as he walked over toward a door at the end of one wall. On the door was a simple sign: *Storage*. Next to it was a keypad.

"This is a very sophisticated pad for a storage room. It requires both a code and facial recognition. We have checked the area on the ground outside this wall. The room is about fifteen feet wide and more than forty feet long, the size of two large containers. The roof lies a foot underground. There is sophisticated air handling equipment, HEPA filters, and humidity and temperature controls. Here on the side, you see heavy power lines going into the room. This is more than a storage room. From its size, it could be the data center for a large international corporation. If this is their data center, we could find all the answers here."

Linda stood silent for a moment. Then she said, "I pray you are right. Get the guys here tomorrow and let them know that the lock may also be armed. Let's call it a day, Steve. Deputy Darby has already set up the security for the night."

Chapter 7

Alex woke up disturbed by some horrible nightmare and totally disoriented. He looked around the semi-dark room and saw another bed and a woman's hair sticking out. The shock made him jump off the bed before he realized where he was and that he was still dressed. He lay back on the bed and thought through the past ten days. As he recalled the shootings, first at the ski hut, then at the B&B, and finally yesterday at the compound, he wished the nightmare back. It was a sweet dream compared to reality.

Then he thought about Alina and the day they had spent together. She was a remarkable woman. In just another day, she would be off to her uncle.

He quietly got up and went to the bathroom with his comb and toothbrush. It was past seven in the morning. They had slept a solid nine hours, and he still felt he could sleep some more.

The shower was refreshing, at first cold to wake him up, then hot to try and clean his body from all the dust and gun smoke he felt covered him. It took a good ten minutes. When he finally went back into the room, he met a smiling, attractive lady sitting in a chair, dressed in light blue pajamas. She had pulled the drapes, and bright sunshine was flooding the room. She was the first to speak.

"Good morning, young man. I was afraid you fell asleep in there. How do you feel this beautiful morning?"

"I feel pretty good for an old man, but I wouldn't mind staying here another day and just going back to sleep. And how are you? Did you sleep well, or have you been pacing the corridors all night?"

"This is the best sleep I've had since I was a kid back home. But sorry, I'd better get into that steam room before it cools down."

With that, she went into the bathroom, and Alex noticed that steam was hanging thick in the air. He sat down to think about this new day. That didn't last long. Alina had left all her clothing on a chair. She would soon come out and get dressed right in front of him. That would be very uncomfortable. He jumped up.

"Alina, I'll go down and check the breakfast room. Are you OK here?"

"Yes, I am. Can you bring me a cup of coffee, please, if it's not too much trouble?"

"Of course. Cream and sugar?" he asked.

"Just black is fine."

"OK, I'll be right back."

He had to run down, get the coffee, and get back to the room, hopefully before she got out of the bathroom. It worked. She was still in the bathroom when he got back, and he told her he would wait for her downstairs. He left quickly so he wouldn't hear any objections or questions.

The TV in the breakfast room was on, and the burning car was still the breaking news. He had heard it all before. So far, so good.

Alina came down after about fifteen minutes, and they had a nice, leisurely breakfast together. Alex couldn't help noticing that she drew the attention of male patrons around the room. That might have been a positive thing under different circumstances. Now it was not, and there was nothing he could do about it.

They got back on the road by 8:30. Destination Seattle. It would be a full day's drive, and they had a late start. Alina insisted on driving. They were both rested, and the car had not yet been identified. Alex felt relaxed compared to yesterday, and he had an interesting travel companion. He had a question.

"Alina, your uncle in Vancouver, is he the father of your cousin here?"

"No. Tanya—that's her name—is my mother's sister's daughter. My uncle in Vancouver, Igor, is my father's brother. He has two sons but no daughters. He was always very good to me. He told me he would like me to be his daughter. I like him a lot. You two would get along very well. But I think I told you; he is very fat and not an athlete at all."

Alex thought about what she said and everything they had talked about.

"It's funny," he started. "Right now, at 9:30, it's been exactly twenty-four hours since we met. It feels so much longer with everything that happened. And we have spent all that time together, night and day. It feels like I have started to get to know you. But that's probably an illusion. Well, I would enjoy meeting your uncle Igor. With his line of work, he must have a lot of interesting stories."

Alina was silent for a minute. Then she said, "Tell me about that illusion."

Alex was taken aback. Illusion? Then he remembered. *Damn*, he thought. *I have to be careful with this lady. And we have at least twelve hours in this car. And maybe another night.*

He answered carefully, "Well, I meant it's easy to get the wrong impression in such a short time. Maybe if I told your uncle Igor what I thought about you, he would totally disagree. 'That's not Alina at all,' he might say. 'Nobody is that perfect.'"

Again, a big laugh, then she said, "I like your company. You are very predictable and very unpredictable. This morning, I knew you would leave the room when I came out to get dressed. I appreciate that a lot. We are not shy in Russia, with saunas and all, but I appreciate that you are so respectful. And then you go and shoot four people, just like that. I was totally shaken. I've been trying to figure out what kind of person can be so different from one minute to the next."

"Well, Alina, if it makes you feel any better, I ask myself the same thing. I have never before hurt a person. The only thing I can come up with to explain what happened is how I reacted when that man kidnapped my grandson. It was a rage I never thought I was capable of. Totally animalistic. And it includes that whole organization. And it's not over. I think this rage will last as long as I live. If I run into anybody associated with that kidnapping group, I will kill them. I can't help it. Life in prison is not a deterrent." Alex took a pause. Alina could sense he was not finished, that he needed to talk, and she was pleased he shared his turmoil with her.

"I don't know how this will evolve over time—if it will fade away or if it will hunt me and drive me nuts. Right now, I feel as good as ever. But here are two things that bother me. You are the only person besides me who knows what's going on here. And I hope you will respect my wish that you will never share this with anybody, at least as long as I live. Tied to that is that you are the only person I can talk to about it. So, when you asked me yesterday to be your friend and support person if you came here, I was happy. It's something I would want from you as well."

Both Alina and Alex sat silent for a while. Finally, she spoke.

"I don't think we have any problem. I have no idea who shot those people. We just traveled together, and I didn't see any shootings. And by the way, I don't for my life believe you are capable of shooting anything. And about the future, I already said I hope to come and live in the US. Maybe I'll get a teaching job close to a ski area. If you call and want to talk, we'll get together, and maybe we can have dinner also."

"That, I would like a lot." They drove on in silence.

After several minutes, Alex asked, "Did you ever see any young children around the place where you and your cousin worked?"

Alina glanced at him. She understood why he asked.

"There was a nursery in the building. It was for people who worked there and also for people who lived in the area. And I don't think any of the people who worked there had any kids, so it was a bit weird. It was in a separate part of the building that you only could enter from the back. I was only in there once. They were kind of by themselves."

She got quiet. Alex looked over and saw tears forming in her eyes. He got his answer. He told her to turn off and park by the side of the road. By the time she stopped the car, tears were rolling down her cheeks. But he also thought he saw something else. Anger. Then she spoke again, with the tears flowing.

"They sometimes had children staying there for several days. They lived there. They told us they were children who lost their parents in accidents and had nobody to take care of them. They were waiting for a foster home. And I believed them."

She opened the door and vomited. Alex got around the car to help her out. He gave her some paper tissues and walked her back around, away from traffic. There was not much to say; they had figured it all out. He handed her a water bottle and helped her into the car. He gave her a little hand squeeze and said,

"It's over now, at least for you. There's not much we can do except contact the authorities—in this case, the FBI. Several local cops are in on this. But first, can you call your cousin? If she is the one to contact the FBI, she will be a hero, not an accomplice."

"What is the FBI?" Alina asked.

"It's our federal police. They deal with crimes that cover several states and a lot of other stuff. They step in when local police cannot handle a situation, they don't have the resources, or when it's out of their jurisdiction. They are right now involved in this kidnapping investigation. I got that on the news a couple of days ago. A lady in Denver, Linda Crawford, is in charge. We can get her number if I can use your phone." Alex still thought it was too risky to use his own phone. He did not want to be linked to any part of the mess he was in.

Alina handed over her phone, and Alex got the number to the Denver FBI office. He wrote it down and handed the phone back to Alina.

"You think you can call your cousin?" he asked.

"I don't know. I can call and tell her that the whole operation is criminal. I'll tell her that law enforcement, including the FBI, will soon move in and that she has to get out of there. See what she says. If she is surprised and doesn't know anything, then I'll ask her to call the FBI. You think that can work?"

"It might work. Go ahead and try. Can you put your phone on speaker?"

Alina looked at Alex for a second, and then she made the call. There were several rings before her cousin answered in a very agitated voice.

"Alina, where are you? Are you OK? It's just chaos here. People are dead, and I am so scared. I don't know what to do. I have no car; somebody took it. Can you come and pick me up?"

Alex gave Alina the note with the FBI number.

Alina said, "Tanya, listen carefully. I cannot come there; I'm in another state. We have been working for a crime organization. It's falling apart. You have to make a call right now to a policewoman in Denver. Tell her everything and tell her you need help. You are in danger. Her name is Linda Crawford. Here is her number. Write it down. You call her, and you will be fine. I'll see you soon. Love you. Bye-bye."

She ended the call and looked at Alex. The time was exactly 10:42 a.m.

He gave her an appreciative nod and said, "Very good. Now we can only wait and see what happens."

Alina sat silent, deep in thought, trying to get a grip on the whole situation and the role she and her cousin had played in it. How could she have been so blind and so naïve not to suspect anything? Nothing at all? She felt both guilty and deceived. She had been a facilitator of a horrible crime, unknowingly. That was a lame excuse in her eyes. She wanted to scream in complete frustration.

They drove on. The next major city would be Boise, and they should be there by early afternoon. It could be a good place to stop for a late lunch. Then, on toward Seattle. The weather was still sunny, but clouds had started to build over the last hour. To reach their destination before nightfall would be a stretch, even under the best conditions.

After a while, Alex glanced over at Alina. She was asleep. *Good*, he thought. *That will help her regain her balance and upbeat spirit*. He decided to drive as long as she was sleeping.

About an hour later, as they approached Boise and the traffic got busier, Alina woke up. After a moment of confusion, she got her bearings and looked over at Alex.

"Why did you let me sleep when we're traveling through this beautiful part of the country? I've been looking forward to seeing it so much!"

Alex couldn't suppress a smile. The lady was back.

After a few miles they came upon a service plaza. Alex spotted an IHOP and turned into the parking lot.

"What kind of restaurant is this *IHOP*?" Alina asked.

"Best restaurant in the world. The International House of Pancakes. It has been my favorite since I was a kid. But don't worry, they have a lot more than pancakes on the menu. And then, from here on, you can be the driver and enjoy every mile of the rest of our drive while I take my beauty nap."

"Thanks a lot. I bet when we get back in the car, the rain will be pouring down."

"Well, you win some and you lose some, as we say here. I'm sure you will do just fine. From what I've seen, you are a very good driver. Now, let's get a table and check the menu."

The rain started when they were halfway through their lunch. By the time they paid the bill, they heard the first cracks of thunder. They ran back to the car as fast as they could and were soaking wet when they shut the doors. They looked at each other and laughed. It was a refreshing and relaxing laugh, the first in a long while for both. That's when they discovered that they had jumped back into their old seats. Alex was again the driver.

"Well, you win some, you lose some," Alina said with a sympathetic smile.

Alex chuckled. "I'm getting a feeling you don't have much experience when it comes to losing. But regardless of who is driving, we are not going anywhere in this weather. So, let's make some use of the time. I have something else to talk to you about. It's another side of me that I'm not very proud of."

Alina looked at Alex with a curious expression. He continued, "When I shot the three people in the B&B and was getting ready to leave, I saw a leather bag about the size of a briefcase on the kitchen counter. I hadn't seen it before and decided to look inside. I don't know why. Curiosity, maybe.

"Anyway, the bag was full of money, neatly packed. I decided to take part of it. The only explanation is what I felt when I stood there, that this money wasn't theirs in the first place. When this is all over, I will hand over the money—or rather, what is left of it— to the FBI. I have no idea what lies ahead for us and what expenses we may have, and I have no problem using that money to escape the people who want us dead.

"Now some practicalities. First, I need to count the money so I can give a report to the FBI on what I took and what we spent. Then we'll divide it into two bags; we'll put one in your duffel and the other in my backpack. And that's for safety. If we get separated, or, God forbid, I get shot, you have money to help you move on. And to remove some of the goodwill I may have built with you, the gas money I gave you didn't come from me; it came from your employer. I thought maybe you'd like to know that."

Alina chuckled, shook her head a little, and just sat silent, contemplating what she had just heard. After some time, she spoke. "You are the most complex person I've met or heard of. Not only for saving people one moment and killing people the next but also for stealing money and then giving it away. What else do you do? Can't you give me the whole list and be done with it, or do you think that would scare me away? If that's the case, you're wrong. I enjoy every minute with you."

"Sorry if I disappoint you. The truth is that I am a very straight and boring person. I have no hidden agenda or secrets. I pay my taxes on time and follow the law. Well, so far anyway. But hey, the rain has almost stopped. If you really want to drive, we can switch. A few more drops won't kill us. Then I will start counting the loot. No talking and no driving instructions."

Alina agreed. They ran around the car, almost colliding midway. They shared a quick hug and a laugh in the rain. They started to travel west as the rain-soaked interstate kept the traffic speed down to well below the limit.

Chapter 8

The helicopter showed up at 8:30 Thursday morning. With it were Susan, Agent Conner, two lock specialists, and two explosives specialists—a full load. There had not been room for two extra agents to accompany the arrested deputy to Denver, and separate transportation had been arranged for him. With no other flights scheduled, the pilot stayed around.

The four specialists went to work, first on the safe, which took them about a half hour. Then they went down to the game room. Steve explained what they had discovered, including the ventilation equipment, and what they hoped to find inside.

After examining the keypad and discussing what they believed was hidden behind it, the head of the group, Walter Langer, summarized the situation. This was an unusual and quite complex lock system. There was no way of telling if the system was armed. The specialists had a methodology of going about the job so as not to cause any explosions, outside or inside. It was a time-consuming process; they estimated it would take between four hours and two days. Only the four of them were allowed in the building as the work progressed.

Linda ordered two deputies to keep the house off-limits to any other person until the four guys showed up, either for a break or because the job was done. Without access to the main building, they became a bit handicapped. Most of their work, including their meetings, had taken place inside the white mansion. Steve suggested they go over to the man cave and talk things over. They were still in an active crime scene, so all they could do was sit in the chairs and talk. They couldn't even brew coffee.

They were still in the process of getting adjusted to the new situation when Linda's phone rang. It was just before eleven in the morning, and the call was forwarded from the Denver office. It meant that the call had gone through the first screening.

"Agent Crawford," Linda answered.

A very excited woman was on the line. Linda put the phone on speaker.

"Oh, Agent Crawford, my name is Tanya. I work here, but now everybody has disappeared and died. I am so scared. I don't know what is going on. Can you help me, please?" The woman was hysterical. She had an accent, maybe Eastern European. Linda tried to calm her.

"Tanya, we will come and help you. But we must know where you are. Can you give me an address, at least a street and town?"

"Yes, yes, I'm in Eagle—no, Avon, and the street is Mountain Brush. I don't know the number. A big yellow building."

Linda was spinning her finger in the air as she talked. George ran out and hollered at the pilot to get ready. Six agents quickly gathered their equipment, protective jackets, helmets, and weapons and were ready for takeoff in a couple of minutes.

Linda was still on her phone as she walked toward the helicopter. She looked agitated as she told the woman to go outside with a white towel and wave when she saw a helicopter coming in maybe ten minutes. She ended the call and gave the pilot the street name. Then she sat back, put the seat belt on, and said with a grim face, "There are two young children at the place." She closed her eyes for a moment as the chopper took off. Then she contacted the pilot.

"Captain, we need two ambulances and a pediatric doctor. Can you call and have them follow us to the house?"

"Roger that," he confirmed.

It was a fifteen-minute ride. The pilot maneuvered the helicopter to the street and then followed it up the mountain. The two ambulances followed at a growing distance on the very curvy road. The pilot spotted the house and the woman with the towel. He put the helicopter down on an open spot in front of the building. The six agents disembarked as soon as they were on the ground and ran toward the crying woman. While still in motion, Linda shouted, "Where are the children?"

That brought some sense to the woman, who immediately started to run around the building and opened a door on the side.

"They are in here. I think they are sleeping." Tanya pointed toward two bundles lying motionless on two beds.

The place was filthy beyond anything Linda had seen. They heard the ambulances approaching. Linda told one of the agents to meet the ambulances and the doctor and another to take Tanya outside and try to calm her.

The doctor who jumped out of the first ambulance immediately asked who was in charge. Her voice had an authority that defied her appearance. She looked like a pretty Latina teenager. One of the agents pointed toward the back door and told her that Agent Linda Crawford was in charge, and she was in that room with the children. The young doctor was already halfway toward the door, carrying a sizeable satchel, and was followed by a medic, who carried two large bags.

Two stretchers were pulled out of the ambulances by a couple of medics. They followed the doctor into the room. Inside the poorly lit room, Linda met the doctor.

"I'm Special Agent Linda Crawford. Go right ahead, Doctor." She pointed toward the two beds.

"I'm Dr. Lopez. Can we get more light in here?"

The medic was already pulling some lamp-like device out of one bag and setting it up over the nearest bed. Within seconds, the doctor had her stethoscope and a headlamp ready and bent down over the little, motionless child. She gave some instructions to the medic, who supplied her with an oxygen tank and an injection needle. The doctor held the oxygen mask over the face of the child as she checked her heart. She then took some time to find a vein in the tiny arm to start an intravenous line. The child was moved from the bed to one of the stretchers. The doctor checked the child carefully again before telling the medics to load the stretcher into the ambulance. The procedure was repeated with the second child.

Both stretchers fit into one ambulance, and the doctor and two medics got in for the ride to the hospital. Before they closed the doors, the doctor looked at Linda and said, "Call me in an hour. We should have a prognosis then." Linda was both impressed and relieved.

The second ambulance was still waiting for instructions. Linda asked the driver to wait; they had one more patient. She found the agent and Tanya sitting on a bench, talking. Tanya had made an impressive recovery. Linda asked her what she was doing at this location and also asked her to show them around. They walked around the building, office area, and living quarters while Tanya told her story.

"After high school, I studied economics and then got a job as an accountant with a company in Moscow, where we lived. During the summer holidays, I traveled, mostly in Europe. Then one summer, I applied for a tourist visa to the USA. I liked it a lot here and decided to try to get a work visa for a year. To get one, you must have a job offer. One of the friends I made here lives in Colorado, and she helped me find this job. It took a few months to get the visa, and I was very excited when I got it. It was renewed almost a year ago, so I will have to return home in a couple of months."

Linda said, "OK, and what can you tell me about the business, what you did here?"

Tanya thought for a moment, then said, "Early on, we had two businesses, the daycare and a B&B. I did the bookkeeping for both. We had a few children in the daycare from families in the area, but they didn't pay anything. The owner donated the money, which I booked as income. Same thing with the B&B. We never charged the guests, but we booked income that the owner donated. He was a very generous man. After about a year, the children didn't come anymore. Maybe they were older and there were no new babies in the area. We only had a couple of temporary children who had lost their parents and were waiting for a foster home.

"That was also when two guys moved in and a couple of girls were let go. That's also when they started to give us drugs for free. They said it would help sharpen our minds. They asked me already after I started here to try and find a Russian friend who wanted to work here. They said they liked us, that we were hardworking and not complaining. I contacted my cousin Alina, and she was interested and came here about four or five months ago. She is the one who called and told me to call you."

Tanya got silent. Linda thought for a moment and said, "Thank you very much, Tanya. That explains a lot. And the B&B, is that where the car exploded?"

"No, it's about an hour from here. It's open during the summer, and we have many guests there. To get there, we drive past Vail; then, on top of the pass, where there is an Indian museum, we turn off on a small road for about a mile. It's very isolated and beautiful there."

"Thanks again, Tanya. We will let you go with the ambulance now and get a checkup at the hospital. I will get in touch with you later and talk more. Thank you so much for your help." Linda turned to the medic. "Can you bring Tanya back to the hospital for evaluation? Make sure she is safe and isolated until an FBI agent comes for her. She is an important and therefore at-risk witness."

She told two agents to stay at the site to search and secure the building. She then went back to the other agents, Steve, George, and Bob, who were waiting by the helicopter with the pilot.

"We have a lead," she opened. "A B&B about a mile from the Native American museum on top of Vail Pass. Captain, you think you can find that for us?"

The pilot was already working his pad. It took him less than two minutes to find the B&B and to tell Linda he could have them there in fifteen minutes.

"Let's go!" Linda said as all four agents got on board.

The flight was fast, scenic, and filled with anticipation. The pilot put the helicopter down on the open, snow-covered field right outside the property. A black pickup was parked in front of a large building. The four agents disembarked and walked toward the building. As they entered the property, Linda instructed Steve and Bob to stay behind as she and George walked past the black pickup toward the front door. There were prints in the snow from trucks coming and going, as well as footprints and ski tracks.

George rang the bell. They waited a moment, and he rang again, longer this time. They could hear the bell inside; besides that, nothing. George suggested they walk around the building and check the back. Linda checked the door. It was unlocked.

"Let's take a peek first," she said and opened the door. They could see the whole large room from where they stood. They could see a bundle of people lying halfway up the wide staircase. They could see the entire floor covered in blood, all the way from the back and up to the door where they were standing. The blood was black—dry. There was no sound, no movement.

"It looks like three people. How many can you see?" Linda asked.

"I agree. Looks like three," George answered.

"Question is, are there more elsewhere in the house? Maybe somebody is still alive," Linda said as she turned around and waved to the others to join them.

Steve and Bob knew from watching the pair open the door and remain outside that something unusual was going on inside. They were right. They also counted three bodies on the stairs, although, among all the legs and arms, another body may be discovered underneath it all.

"We need to verify that nobody is alive in there, and we cannot step inside here. Let's see if there is another way into the house, maybe a back door or a fire escape," Linda directed. She asked Steve to stay where he was and take as many pictures as possible.

The rest of the agents walked around the building. They found an unlocked door on the ground level, which opened into a small apartment. It was obviously a caretaker's apartment. There was clothing, an open pill bottle—no, two bottles— and two types of pills lying around. Linda and George stood there, trying to make sense of the scene. Finally, Linda took the two empty bottles and all the pills, which she put in one bottle, and said, "We can stand here a week and stare without being any wiser. Let's go."

George opened the door to the great room. The blood had reached the threshold and stopped them from going farther into the house. They still couldn't reach the upper level and continued their outside walk. There were no ladders, but there were a couple of balconies. George ran up front. He had spotted what might be a ladder in the pickup truck. He came back with an eight-footer. It was not long enough for a comfortable climb, but he thought he could make it if they stabilized the ladder as he reached the top steps.

George made it up and then helped Bob to join him. The balcony door was locked, and they had to break a window to get inside. On the inside, they walked the six bedrooms. Nobody was found. They walked out on the landing and counted the people on the stairs. There were three, two men and a woman.

Bob went down the stairs a few steps to get a closer look at the bodies. "Shotgun wounds," he told George.

Then they took pictures of the one bedroom that was stripped of bedding and towels. They went through the Jack and Jill bathroom to the joining bedroom. There they stood for a few minutes, looking through the open door out to the wrap-around landing and the heap of bodies lying on the stairway. Bob broke the silence.

"This guy was expecting those people. He left the other bedroom, where they thought he was sleeping, waited for them in here, and shot them as they came up the stairs. Then he left with all the sheets and towels. The blood had not yet spread all over the floor, so he got out without leaving any tracks. He used a shotgun, and with three people, he probably had to reload. He was standing in here or possibly lying on the floor. Does anything sound familiar?"

"I have nothing to add," George said. "This guy shot these people probably on Tuesday night, then drove down to Eagle and shot the other four yesterday around noon. He killed six people in twelve hours or less. An entire crime gang taken out by one guy and maybe a driver. He knew the people. Must have been an insider. Irony is, he did our job, and now we have to find him and put him away for life. Let's get out of here!" he said with an edge in his voice as they headed back to the balcony.

Down on the ground, George gave Linda the picture. It took less than three minutes. The bottom line was both simple and scary. The same shooter, the same method, the same result, the same day.

"This is for the history books," he joked.

Linda called Tom. He answered with his usual upbeat greeting.

"Hi, Linda, how is your day going so far?"

"I don't know, Tom. You be the judge. We have found two new locations: one with two little kids—three or four years old, unconscious, and now in critical care, with the outcome unknown—and the other with three dead people—two guys and one woman who have been dead for a day or two, probably killed by the same shooter that got the SUV. That's six people shot dead in twelve hours or so. It should be a good day, but it doesn't feel like it. And we need two sanitizing crews," Linda ended her report.

"And why do you think it's the same shooter?" Tom asked.

Linda thought before she answered. "We don't know for sure, but this is what we believe: He's an insider, a vigilante on a mission. He knows their whereabouts and their behavior because he is one of them. And a shotgun was used in both places. We have talked about this and agree that it is not likely that there are two shooters; it'd be too risky that one will turn. And we also think it's a guy because a woman would never get into the inner circle to gather all the knowledge he has."

Tom thought for a moment before he answered. "I cannot remember a day like this. You guys have done a terrific job. I will send up two sanitizing crews right away and six agents tomorrow morning. You hand over, and all five of you come back and spend the weekend with your families. Monday morning, we plan next week. OK?"

"OK, let's plan for that, but we have some very important work going on right now at the mansion. I will leave two agents here now and head back there. I will call you in an hour or so." Linda ended the call.

"You guys stay behind until the sanitizing crew comes up. You can use the apartment for shelter," Linda told George and Bob. She and Steve walked up to the helicopter and asked the pilot to take them back to the compound. But first she called Dr. Lopez. She had to wait a few moments before the doctor answered.

"Hi, Linda. I can only tell you that both girls are alive but very weak. They are in emergency care for now. They were heavily sedated with both legal and illegal drugs. We should know more in three to four hours, and you are welcome to call then."

Thirty minutes later, Linda and Steve were back at the compound. They had been away for three hours, and the entire investigation was shed in a new light. There were a lot of new discoveries but no new answers.

The safe breakers were still at work, and the mansion was off target. Linda told Steve that she needed to talk to him in the man cave. They sat down. Linda thought for a moment before she spoke.

"Steve, the findings today raise a lot of questions in my mind. The girl, Tanya, is from Russia. She said that her cousin had told her to call us and had given her our number. A cousin of a Russian girl, I would think, is Russian. And from the start, we have worked under the assumption that this whole thing is an international crime organization, most likely Russian. Wherever we turn, we are running into Russians. All joking aside, I think we should change our focus and find that Russian cousin. Whatever it takes. It seems to me she is connected. She knows, and she is on our side."

Steve looked at her for a few seconds before he spoke. "I could have started by asking, 'What took you so long?' but that wouldn't be fair. That thought started to form in my mind as we were flying back here. We have to find Tanya's cousin. This afternoon we should go over to the hospital for an interview with Tanya. And at the same time, try and find out if the two little girls fit the profiles of any kidnap victims."

"Thank you, Steve. You save me a lot of talk. Let's see if we can borrow a car for a couple of hours." Linda was already up, heading for the door.

Outside, they ran into José. He looked happy to see Linda.

"Mrs. Crawford, I have been looking for you. When do you think I can talk to María to see how she and Sofía are doing? I am so worried about them."

"Oh José, I'm so sorry, we have been very busy. Do you have time to talk for a few minutes?" Linda asked.

José had time and suggested they go to his apartment next door. Linda followed him inside, while Steve went over to a couple of agents to try and find a vehicle.

After they were seated, Linda said, "José, I am going to try and get María on the line, but first I have a question: What do you know about the B&B over past Vail?"

"A very nice place. Many guests stay there. I go there sometimes and do repairs. Always good food," José answered right away. "Have you visited there?"

"Yes, I have, and it is a very nice place," Linda said. "And have you been to the other place in Avon with the daycare facility?"

"Yes, I have, also to do repair work. Not as nice as the B&B."

"Do you know Tanya over there and her cousin, Alina?"

"Yes, both very nice ladies."

"I only met Tanya. Alina had left, and Tanya didn't know where she was. Do you know what kind of car Alina is driving?"

"Yes, she has different cars: a Toyota pickup truck and also a Ford Explorer."

"Thank you so much, José. Now I will try and get María, and you two can talk as long as you wish."

Linda called the Denver office and got her assistant. She told her what it was about and handed the phone over to José. Linda left the apartment and caught up with Steve. He had found a vehicle, and they could leave when she was ready. She was almost ready; she only had to talk to one of the Glenwood agents. Steve led her back to Roger Smith, the agent he had just talked to.

"Hi, Roger," Linda said. "I have a very important request. We have to find a Russian woman who has been working at the nursery building in Avon. Her name is Alina. She has disappeared and is driving either a Toyota pickup or a Ford Explorer. Both trucks belong to this business. I want you to find the registration number for both, as well as their age and color, OK?"

"No problem, ma'am. I'll have it in twenty minutes or so," Roger said.

Steve took the wheel as they started their drive to Vail Hospital. As they got up on the interstate, he said, "Your friend José really has to earn his privileges."

"Don't we all," Linda said with a smile.

They got to the pediatric clinic, showed their credentials, and asked for Dr. Lopez. The doctor was seeing a patient and would be with them shortly. Linda used the time to check the whereabouts of their other patient, Tanya. She didn't have her full name, but the hospital was small enough to get them to Tanya's ward. A nurse took the call.

"Good afternoon. This is Agent Crawford with the FBI. I am looking for a patient you got in earlier today, a Russian woman by the name of Tanya. Is she available to visit at this time?"

"Tanya is still under evaluation, and it may be some time before we have a full report on her condition," the nurse answered.

"We will come over in about half an hour, and I hope to see her then. Thank you."

Dr. Lopez showed up a few minutes later. She looked agitated.

"Dr. Lopez, thank you for seeing us," Linda greeted her. She was immediately interrupted.

"Linda, I am Sara to you; I feel we are in this mess together. These little girls are still in emergency care. It looks like they are stabilizing, and I hope they make it through. They are both strong, like they were treated well before they lost their parents, but for about a week or so, it looks as if they have been fed only junk and drugs. What can you tell me about that nursery?"

They were still standing in the hallway, and Linda asked if they had a private room. Sara looked surprised but took them into a small examination room.

"This conversation is confidential. We are not done with our investigation yet, but we believe that the two girls have not lost their parents at all. The parents have lost them," Linda started. "We are looking into a string of kidnappings over several months. The group that held these girls is at the center of that investigation. We have to ask you for a physical description of the two girls—age, size, weight, teeth, eye color, hair color, any birthmarks—so we can see if they match any of the kidnapped children's descriptions."

The young doctor looked at Linda, speechless for a moment. Then she asked, "Does this have anything to do with the shootings yesterday?"

"Yes, it does." Linda nodded.

"Thanks for telling me. Saves me the job," Sara said without a hint of a smile. "I can have the descriptions in an hour, and I hope by then I can make a more definitive prognosis. Thank you, Linda, for sharing that with me."

Linda and Steve walked through the hospital to the internal medicine ward and walked up to the nurses' desk.

"Good afternoon. I am Agent Crawford, and this is Agent Callahan. We are with the FBI, and we're here to see the doctor in charge of Tanya, a Russian woman who came in a few hours ago."

"Yes, we were expecting you. Dr. Black is still tied up with the evaluation, but it should be completed within a half hour or so. You can use the room right behind you while you wait."

They thanked the nurse and walked toward the room. Linda caught a glance at a clock over her head. It was 5:36 p.m. *If every day was like this, I would be ready to retire in a month or less*, she thought. Linda called Tom, who was in his office.

"Good afternoon, Tom, just a quick update. The two little girls we found are alive but very weak. They are in intensive care, and we should know in the morning what their outlook is. Tanya, the Russian woman who took us to them, is still in evaluation here, but I'm not concerned about her. She's shaken up, of course, but seems strong. She gave me an interesting picture of what has happened here over the last couple of years. It seems like they started to plan this kidnapping business about a year ago.

"Another thing Steve and I talked about is her and her cousin, Alina. Behind everything that's happened so far—shootings, FBI alert, children found—the two Russian cousins have been involved. Without them, we would all be sitting around staring at the walls. Tanya is at the hospital here, but we don't know anything about Alina. Our best guess is that she is driving a car belonging to this organization. And Alina was the one who called Tanya and gave her the FBI number and told her to call me. That would suggest she is not alone. Somebody gave her that number. A major problem is that Alina is as valuable to the other side as she is to us. With a general Amber Alert, or any alert for that matter, we issue a death sentence on the woman."

Linda stopped talking, waiting for Tom's response. It took a while before he spoke.

"Those two Russian cousins are our friends, and under no circumstances do we put them at risk. Also, to protect them we must keep their names from the media. They have to be given the highest security. This also brings up another issue for us. If we have any proof that this whole operation is run by a crime organization based in a foreign country, our director has an obligation to brief the White House, then give a status report every Monday morning at nine o'clock wherever in the world POTUS happens to be. When does our belief become conviction, Linda?"

"We are not there yet, but as soon as we have one piece of proof, you will know."

"Thank you. You are doing a stellar job. And those two little girls, I really hope they will do well. Call me later with the doctor's report, OK?"

"Will do, Tom. Goodbye."

Linda hung up and turned to Steve, who had a quizzical expression on his face.

"He said not to put any of the cousins at risk and to protect their names by giving them the highest security. He also said that our director has to inform the president if we have proof that this operation is run by a foreign-based crime organization. Now we have to come up with a way to find Alina without going out with a search. Any ideas?"

Dr. Black came out to their waiting area, interrupting their talk. He was a middle-aged man, looked fit and confident, and suggested they go to his office down the hall.

"The woman that came in earlier, Tanya, is in a difficult position," Dr. Black began. "She has been using drugs, primarily opioids, for a couple of years. The first and most obvious step is to put her in rehab, but the problem with that is that she does not have any support group around here. We can take care of the initial phase of the program. We're talking about five to seven days of heavy detox, but beyond that, she should join a normal program.

"From what she told me, she is here on a one-year work visa, which has been renewed once. That will probably not happen again, so her return home to Russia would be a logical next step. Besides her drug problem, she seems to be in good physical health. Mentally, she is in a state of shock after the last couple of days. All the people around her, including a cousin, just disappeared. She said she found two very young children in a nursery in the building when she was looking for her friends. I guess you know all about that. The bottom line is, we need to keep her through the shock stage at least till this coming Monday and preferably all of next week. Then we can talk again. Any questions?"

Linda answered, "Yes, Doctor, but first we have to share some confidential information with you. This woman, Tanya, is one of our key witnesses against a widespread international crime organization dealing in human trafficking, drugs, and kidnappings. She has been given the highest security level and will be in the custody of the FBI until this whole thing has been put to bed. One month, two years—whatever it takes.

"As a key witness, she is at extremely high risk, and her name must be kept under cover. We have had a lot of activity in the last two days, with six people, all part of this crime organization, shot dead. Behind all the shootings, we see some kind of participation by two women: Tanya here, and her cousin Alina. We do not know where Alina is, and our most pressing task right now is to find her alive. We appreciate your suggestion to keep Tanya here until Monday, and we will bring in around-the-clock security. The alternative is to bring her down to Denver tomorrow. Any thoughts on your part, Doctor?"

The doctor thought for a moment. "The picture you just painted puts Tanya in a new light. I will spend the weekend reviewing her case and consulting with some rehab specialists. By Monday, I hope to present a program that will be appropriate for Tanya and for the FBI. We will also move her to a different room that's more appropriate from a security aspect. I believe she will feel comfortable here for a week or so. We'll also immediately protect her name and identity."

Linda stretched out her hand. "Thank you, Dr. Black. We look forward to seeing you Monday."

Linda and Steve left the room and walked into the hallway, over to the nurse they had talked to earlier. They asked if it was OK for them to see Tanya. The nurse said she would check and walked over to one of the rooms. After a few moments, she came out and waved them in.

Tanya was sitting in a chair, flipping through a magazine. There was little resemblance with the disheveled, panicky woman they had met the same morning. She was an attractive, smiling, thirty-something woman, looking like she was waiting for a date to take her out. Both Linda and Steve broke out in broad smiles.

"Hi, Tanya, you look a world better than when we met this morning!" Linda greeted her. "This is Steve Callahan, and I am Linda Crawford. We are both with the FBI. We are just saying hi to let you know that we are around and will come and talk to you whenever you wish. How do you feel right now?"

"I feel fine, but I am very concerned about my cousin, Alina. Do you know anything about her?"

"No, we have no news about Alina. When was the last time you talked to her or saw her?"

"It was this morning, around ten o'clock, I think. She called me and told me to call you. She gave me your number and said you would help me. She also said we had been working for a crime organization, and it was falling apart."

"The good news is that she called you and gave you all that information," Linda started. "That means she is safe, not running or held against her will. It also sounds like she is not alone. Somebody gave her that information and my telephone number. We don't know where she is, but we know she is OK. Have you tried to call her?"

"I can't find my phone. I have looked through my things. Maybe I lost it up by the house this morning."

"Let us have the number and we will try and locate it," Linda said.

Tanya gave her the number as Steve called one of the agents they had left at the house. He asked if they had found any cell phones lying around. They had not, and Steve gave him Tanya's number. They would call back when they found the phone.

Linda informed Tanya that she was a very important witness against the criminal organization she had unknowingly worked for. She also informed her about the talk she had had with Dr. Black. For Tanya's safety, they would provide security around the clock. It also meant that she could not move around by herself; she always had to have a guard.

"Sometimes," Linda said, "there's not much of a difference between the good guy and the bad guy. They both have to be guarded but for different reasons."

"I am glad I don't have to worry about those people anymore," Tanya said.

Linda and Steve wished her a good night and left. It was past seven, and there was still some work to be done. They walked back to the pediatric ward to see Dr. Lopez. She had left for the day but had prepared a report, which the nurse handed over.

Linda immediately opened the envelope. First was a summary of the girls' conditions, which had stabilized to the point where they were no longer in a high-risk condition. They were still weak and would be kept in intensive care over the weekend. There was also one sheet for each of them with all their personal data. That would be all they needed to match the girls with their parents. Linda was excited as they drove back to the compound and called Tom with the good news.

By the time they arrived at the mansion, the four lock experts had just finished the day but were still not done. They would be back early in the morning and would hopefully finish the job by midday. They had strict work rules, for good reason.

Linda found Agent Smith. He had the vehicle information she had asked for. The pickup truck was a three-year-old gray Toyota Tacoma, and the Ford Explorer was brown and four years old. He also gave her the license numbers. Linda thanked him and walked over to Steve, who was talking to a couple of night guards. When he was finished, she told him they had the vehicle information and needed to talk about the search for Alina. She suggested they talk about it over dinner.

Steve asked one of the agents to drive them back to the hotel. There was no need to have a car sitting idle all night, and there were restaurants within walking distance. They were dropped off outside a steakhouse. They both realized how starving they were after twelve hours just on water and some snacks. They got a table and ordered wine and food, steak for Steve and salmon for Linda. When the waiter had brought the two wine glasses, Linda brought up the topic of the dinner conversation: how to deal with the Alina situation. It had been bothering her all day somewhere in the back of her head.

Steve looked at her for a moment, then said, "You know Linda, sometimes, when you are not certain what to do, the best course of action is to do nothing. Leave it be. Eventually, things might happen that will call for action, and then you will know what to do. We have had an incredibly productive day. This kind of day is what memories and careers are made of. Let's relax and enjoy dinner. And cheers to this day and to you. It's a pleasure working for you!" They both smiled as they sipped the wine.

"Thank you for that advice. I feel a lot better," Linda said. "I also appreciate you being here to catch me when I stumble. And I will never forget today, the mystery of the two Russian ladies who seem to point us where to go every step of the way. Someday we may have all the answers.

"And then again, we may not," Steve said. "It may be an unanswered riddle you can think about and write a book about in retirement."

They both laughed just as the waiter brought their food.

Chapter 9

The money in the bag was all sorted and bundled as if it came straight from the bank. Alex counted a total of twenty bundles of twenty-, fifty-, and hundred-dollar bills. He quickly checked that each bundle held only one currency. A value was written on the wrapping, and Alex decided to count a few bundles to verify that the values were correct. The wrappings could be reused or deliberately mismarked. There were eight bundles with $100 bills, three with $50 bills, and nine with $20 bills. If the markings on the wrappings were correct, the total was $113,000—a staggering amount!

First, he had to determine from which bundle he had pulled the money he gave Alina and how much they had spent so far. He had paid for their hotel and meals out of his own wallet, and he planned to reimburse himself once he added up the total. It was a bit time-consuming to sit in the front seat of a moving pickup and count all the banknotes. There were a few discrepancies, but after re-counting them, they all were according to their labels, except for the twenty-four $20 bills he had given Alina.

"Done," Alex said as he set up and looked out the window for the first time in over an hour. "Now I only need another plastic bag for your share. We will not reach Seattle today, so we can take care of that later. It's already a quarter to six, and I need to find a news station."

Alex got busy with the dial and found a station in a couple of minutes. Another phony pharma commercial was broadcast at the moment. He turned it down to the lowest volume he could still hear so he wouldn't miss the news.

"Are you satisfied with your first attempt as a robber?" Alina asked with a smile.

"More than satisfied. I think we are the modern Bonnie and Clyde. But then again, they both died at the end, so we must scrap that," Alex chuckled.

"Who are Bonnie and Clyde?" Alina asked.

"I'll tell you later. The news is on," Alex said as he turned up the volume.

The newscast opened with breaking news, which was all about the explosion in Colorado. There was room for little else. The FBI had arrived on the scene yesterday at midafternoon. State troopers, together with the sheriff and several deputies, had been on site since the explosion. Several officers had been on site all night. A few hours ago, right around 11:00 a.m., six officers in full battle gear had taken off in an FBI helicopter for an undisclosed destination. No information as to why or where had been given.

"Thank you, Tanya," Alina whispered.

The rain was not going to ease up any time soon. Instead, it intensified and started to be uncomfortable. They were moving at about fifty miles per hour, with splashes drowning the entire pickup every so often. Alex suggested they stop at the next hotel and have a nice dinner. There were no objections from the driver.

It didn't take long before they came to a service plaza with several hotels and restaurants. Alex went to the first one and got a room. He told the front desk agent that they would start with dinner and asked for a steakhouse nearby. The best was an Applebee's just down the road. That would do fine; a steak and a glass of wine were all that mattered at this point.

The restaurant was not crowded, probably because of the weather. Alex and Alina ordered their steaks and wine, and as before, Alina played the role of a normal American wife perfectly. They made small talk, sipped their wine, laughed on occasion, and fit right in. Some of the men glanced over occasionally. *Lucky guy*, their eyes said.

They finished with Alina's favorite dessert, key lime pie with whipped cream. Alex felt totally comfortable, relaxed, and, yes, *happy* in the company of this remarkable Russian lady. It bugged him a bit. It wasn't in his plan.

The rain was coming down hard, and they unloaded under the hotel's porte cochere, where Alina and the luggage stayed dry. Alex drove the pickup far away from the entrance and parked with the lone license plate against a wall. In spite of his best effort to hold a poncho tight around his body, he was soaked as they entered the hotel. A hot shower was only minutes away, so being wet didn't bother him at all. What bothered him were a couple of issues he and Alina needed to talk about.

The first thing Alex did in the room was to get the shower going and get out of his wet clothes. He had a long, hot shower and felt refreshed and rejuvenated when he stepped into the room. Alina smiled at him.

"Wow, you look good. What did you do in there? Tell me, a secret shampoo, or what?"

"Well, Alina, if anything affects me one way or another, it's you. It's rather amazing. When I woke up yesterday morning, I didn't even know you existed, and here we are, a day later, having dinner like a normal married couple. And I like it. Every minute with you is an adventure. Our problem is that we are both running, and we are running from both the bad guys and the good guys without knowing which is which. Today, I had expected to hear about a search for the pickup. It didn't happen. Maybe they have some new methods I am not familiar with, or they decided to let us be. We don't know.

"Our goal is to get you to your uncle in Vancouver without a passport. The only way I see how to do that is to get a boat, as we talked about yesterday. We have enough money, and the best place is somewhere between Portland and Seattle. What I suggest is we drive to Seattle, go to the biggest marina, and look for boats for sale. But first, you have to talk to your uncle and make sure this works for him. You think you can call him in the morning?"

"You know," Alina said, "it's been so much fun driving around with you, so I stopped thinking about reality. But yes, I can call him in the morning. And what if he says no?"

"We'll cross that bridge when we get there, as we say here. And worst case, I may have to adopt you." Another big belly laugh from Alina.

"If that's the worst case, why even waste money on a call?" When she wiped her eyes, she said she would call after breakfast.

Their talk about reality seemed to dampen Alina's mood. They both got ready for bed, with due respect for their privacy. Alex was done in the bathroom and went to bed first. He chose the bed away from the bathroom, by the window. As Alina came out and was ready, she walked over to Alex's bed and looked at him.

"Alex, I feel so lonely. Can you hold me for just a minute?"

"Of course," Alex said, opening the covers for her. "My grandchildren ask me that all the time."

Alina crawled inside the covers. They both wrapped their arms around each other. For Alex, the feeling of an adult, attractive woman in his arms was something he had forgotten over the years since he lost his wife. He was not comfortable, and he tried to push his thoughts toward the boat he was going to buy the next day.

After no more than a minute, he could feel Alina's breathing and body relaxing. She had fallen asleep, just like his grandchildren did. And what was he going to do? He could try and sneak out into the other bed. That's what he would do. But first, he would stay a little longer to make sure Alina was deep asleep and didn't wake up.

* * *

Alex opened his eyes and saw the morning sun between the drapes. But that was not what woke him up. Alina was still lying in his arms. There was a slight movement in her body, a rhythmic movement that slowly increased. Her breathing followed until she suddenly woke up. She was sweaty and disoriented. She looked at Alex and asked, "What happened? What did you do?"

"I did nothing. You were dreaming, little girl. You don't remember?"

"If that was a dream, I want to go back to sleep," she said and kissed Alex—a long lover's kiss, as her hands were all over him. Alex had no strength—or will—to protest. Nature had taken full control of them both.

It was past nine when they got out of bed, both smiling and touching. Alina said, "I'm starving. And for food this time. Do you think it's still time for breakfast?"

"Yes, we have another hour, but we'd better get going or there won't be much left," Alex replied.

They finally came back to earth, showered, dressed, and headed down to the breakfast room. They had lots of coffee, orange juice, eggs, bacon, and muffins; they had huge appetites.

Back in the room, Alex reminded Alina of the call to her uncle. Her happy face turned serious as she was suddenly brought back to reality. It took a while before somebody answered. Alina spoke Russian. The conversation went on for several minutes. She looked a little uncomfortable as she said, "It wasn't my uncle. It was somebody else I talked to. He said they were very busy at the consulate. My uncle is getting ready to leave for Russia next week. He would give him the message to call back but didn't know when that could happen."

"Don't worry. We have about two hours' drive left, and he might call before we get there."

They packed their belongings and checked out. Alex took the wheel, and Alina got in the passenger's seat. They drove the first several miles in silence. The last few hours had brought a change to their relationship, unplanned and surprising. Alina broke the silence.

"This morning was the finest time in my life. You stirred my emotions already on that bench when you talked to me and pushed that water bottle over. I still hope all the things we have talked about—me coming back here, finding a job, and staying in touch with you—will happen."

Alex was relieved by what Alina said. He would not have known how to break the silence. Now that was taken care of in a way that made him feel both comfortable and, again, happy. He reached over, squeezed her hand, and said, "I want the same. Let's make it happen!"

They again drove in silence for quite a while. This time, Alex was the one to start talking.

"I've been thinking about our next step. The FBI did not go out with a search for this car. It looks like they are not anxious to bring you in, for whatever reason. I think we can hang on to the car, at least for now, and use it to look for a boat. It would simplify that process a lot."

About an hour into their journey, Alina's phone rang. She recognized her uncle's number and answered in Russian. They had a long conversation, of which Alex could not understand a word. When it was finally over, Alina looked exhausted, and it took a few moments before she started to translate what had been said.

Some time ago, her uncle had agreed with the Russian State Department to retire as of this Friday. He was several years past the official retirement age, so that was all fine. His replacement had been in place for almost a month. His wife was going to fly back to Moscow this Sunday. He had decided to bring his beloved fishing boat back to Russia and would start that journey in about a week.

He was officially retired, so he was no longer able to issue any visas or passports. The only thing he could offer was to take Alina with him on his boat back to Russia. There was plenty of room, but she had to meet him at least thirty miles offshore so as not to conflict with any immigration rules. She had to let him know in a week if she was interested and if this could be arranged.

"Wow" was Alex's first reaction. He was silent for a while, pondering his response. Thirty miles offshore made no sense when international waters began twelve miles out. He could understand fifteen miles to be on the safe side, but thirty?

Alex did not want Alina to pick up on his concerns. He quickly asked her, "Do you know what kind of fishing boat your uncle has? It must be a ship to travel all the way to Russia."

"I don't know what kind of boat it is, but I think it's big. My father told me my uncle goes out fishing, sometimes for weeks, up around Alaska and down around Central America."

"Sounds like Russian diplomats make a lot more money than their American counterparts. But let's talk about what we are going to do now with this new information. We can still look for a boat. If we can't find one, then the whole plan to meet your uncle is out. If we do find one, then we can think about what we are doing next. We can meet your uncle thirty miles out, and there you can decide whether to travel with him to Russia or just say hi and stay here with me. Of course, once we get back, we still have to figure out how to get you a new passport and a visa to remain in the US, but that's way in the future."

They turned off onto Interstate 82 toward Seattle. There was still well over a three-hour drive left, and they decided to start looking for a break area for lunch and gas.

Alina turned toward Alex. "Who are you visiting in Seattle? A friend, or a relative?"

Alex took a while to answer. "There is nobody in Seattle. When you said you were going to Vancouver, I just came up with Seattle. I had no plan for what to do after the shooting that night. I hadn't even started to think about it. A ride with you would take care of that whole problem and take me out of enemy territory. At the same time, I didn't want to seem too anxious and maybe scare you away, so I let you make the decision. That's what's in Seattle."

Alina looked at Alex. His face was serious with no sign of a smile. "So, you trusted me to come back and pick you up because of your charm and good looks?" she said with a smile.

"No, I didn't trust you to come back at all. I was very happy and relieved when I saw you, both because it solved my problem and also because I simply wanted to keep talking to you. Your story intrigued me." Alex was still dead serious. "And," he said, now with a smile, "now you know the truth, for better or for worse."

"Well, my dear Alex, as far as I am concerned, it's for the better," Alina said as she bent over and kissed his cheek.

They came up on a service plaza. Alex turned off and drove to a gas station. He also bought some water bottles and snacks before they went to one of the restaurants. Alina wanted to try eggs Benedict; the name sounded good. Alex had his usual two eggs, bacon, hash browns, and, of course, a big pot of coffee.

As they waited, he picked up his phone and started to look for marinas in the Seattle area. After a few minutes, he said the largest marina was in a northern suburb called Everett. The second largest seemed to be Shilshole Bay, just northwest of downtown. Alex decided to start with Everett. It was Friday afternoon, and they would have to deal with some heavy after-work traffic, but they still had several hours. With luck, they would be able to reach the marina before dark.

They soon got onto Interstate 90 and arrived at the Port of Everett Marina by late afternoon. Alex stopped the car and just stared out over thousands of masts rising out of the water like a forest of bare trees. He had picked up that this was one of the largest marinas on the entire West Coast, but the sight still surprised him. And the thought of finding a particular boat seemed overwhelming. He decided to start with the harbor master's office. Maybe there was some order in this chaos.

There was. The type and size of boat he was looking for, a sloop between twenty-six and thirty-three feet, had a certain section, and there were only about five hundred of them. He was also told that boats for sale normally had a sign that listed the owner's or broker's telephone number. He could take pictures of those he was interested in and then call for information at his convenience.

Alina stayed behind to check out the stores, restaurants, and hotels as Alex set out on his hunt up and down several docks. There were not many boats that met his criteria, so his hope of finding one started to dwindle. He was well past the midpoint of his walk when he was taking a couple of pictures of a rather small but rugged-looking boat. On a sign was a telephone number and a name, Jorgen. The doors to the cabin were open, and suddenly a young man came up. He looked thirtyish, blond, and slim.

"Are you interested in my boat?" he asked with a broad smile.

"Well, it looks interesting," Alex said. "What can you tell me about it? Like its price, to start with?

"I want $30,000," he said. "It's a fairly old boat, over sixty years, in fact. It was built in Scandinavia. It's solid. I bought it in Hawaii over three years ago and have lived on it since with my fiancée. My name is Jorgen, by the way. Step on board, and I'll tell you all about it."

Alex looked at his watch. It was already past five.

"My name is Mark," he said, not wanting his name out in case it would show up in some newscast. "I am interested and would like to hear more about it, but I have to meet up with my girlfriend by the stores. Can I come back when I find her?"

"No problem," Jorgen said. "See you in a little bit."

Alex found Alina having a drink in the afternoon sun outside a bar, Bluewater Organic Distilling. Not hard to remember. He told her that he had found an interesting boat and wanted her to join him when the owner showed it to him. Alina was happy to be involved, and they walked back to the boat. As they walked along all the docks, Alex told her his name was Mark Walker. The boat would be bought in her name since he had no ID under his fake name. She accepted that without any questions; there were too many things she didn't understand in the US.

As they approached the boat, she saw the name, *Springtime*. She liked it a lot. It described her feelings the last couple of days.

Jorgen was busy in the cockpit and said something into the cabin when he saw them. When they reached the boat, a pretty blonde girl had joined him. Jorgen stepped up and helped Alina on board. Alex followed her, lucky to be wearing his sneakers; it was a big step. Jorgen introduced his fiancée, Lisa, and "Mark" introduced his "fiancée," Alina. She squeezed his hand hard. They sat down in the cockpit, and Alex was the first to speak.

"Thank you, Jorgen, for inviting us. You said when we met that you bought this boat in Hawaii. Does that mean that you and Lisa sailed it all the way here?"

"Yes," he said. "We sailed from Hawaii to the Galapagos. Lisa loved the islands and the animals. We spent four months there and got engaged. Then we sailed to mainland Ecuador, and from there to here with a lot of interesting stops along the way. I don't know all the previous owners, but somebody sailed it from Scandinavia to Hawaii many years ago, so this was a fairly short distance," Jorgen laughed.

Alex got more intrigued the more the young man talked.

"How do you prepare for that kind of adventure? You must have done a lot of sailing before," he asked.

Jorgen smiled again. "Sailing has been my life. I have been fascinated by sailing and sailboats since I was a kid. I don't know why. Nobody in my family was involved in boating. I grew up in a small town in Denmark called Roskilde. They have a Viking ship museum there, and they also build replicas for people who want a Viking ship to sail. They're much smaller than the ships that sailed across the oceans, of course, but identical in shape and built the old way with the same tools and methods the Vikings used. I was fascinated by that whole thing and was hanging around the place all the time.

"When I was old enough, I did any job they thought I could handle. Everyone who worked there was a volunteer, so they didn't do it for money. They also took me out sailing as a deckhand. Through people I met there, I started crewing local sailboats, then bigger and bigger boats. That's how I met a guy whose family owns one of Denmark's largest shipping companies. The family was the biggest donator to the museum, and I had seen him around without knowing who he was. I ended up crewing different boats in different parts of the world for that family for over five years.

"Then, four years ago, when we were sailing in Hawaii, I ran into this beautiful Danish girl. She was working at a resort in Maui. When I told the captain I had found the girl I wanted to marry and had to leave, he asked to meet Lisa. He liked her a lot and congratulated us both. After that, he sent a letter to the owner, who was back in Denmark. The owner sent me a letter congratulating me and said that I would always have a job with the company. It didn't mean so much then, but now it's different.

"I bought this boat with my savings, and we lived on it and worked and sailed around the islands for a couple of years. Then we wanted to see something different and ended up here. And now, we have decided to get married, have a family, and live in Denmark. The day after I sell the boat, we'll fly back home. Now, what can I tell you about the boat?"

"I am still digesting your story. It's fascinating," Alex said. "And about the boat, I am interested in the boat, but I have a problem with the price. I believe we can get a decent boat that will work for us for around $20,000. But we will pay you $22,000 for the boat, subject to inspection, of course. All cash tomorrow."

It was silent for a little bit while Jorgen was considering the proposal.

"No," he said. "I cannot accept that. I believe we can do better."

"OK," Alex said after some thinking, "here is the best we can offer: We will pay $23,000 for the boat, and then $3,000 as an early wedding gift to you and Lisa."

Jorgen gave up a big laugh.

"How can we turn that down? Lisa will chew ME out for the low price and love YOU for the gift. That's really sneaky. What do you say, Lisa?"

"You are right, I don't like the price, but I love the $3,000. And I also love flying home in a couple of days. Once you start thinking about the next step in life, you want it to happen yesterday. I think we should accept the offer."

They all shook hands, and Alex said, "Let's meet in the morning for the inspection. It's almost six o'clock, and we have to find a hotel and a supply store to get some contract forms."

Jorgen said, "That's fine, and if we meet at noon, Lisa and I should be done cleaning the boat. I'm confident she will pass any inspection after all the hours I spent keeping her up to Lisa's standard."

"Oh, don't blame me for being such a perfectionist," Lisa said with a smile. "It's either in your genes or from building those Viking boats with only stone tools."

Jorgen laughed and said, "In Lisa's view, the Stone Age ended around 1950 when her grandfather was born. The good thing is if I miss something, she points it out, and vice versa."

They all laughed. Alina and "Mark" left the boat with good feelings, both about the boat and about the enjoyable Danish couple.

On the way to the car, Alex reminded Alina to call her uncle, tell him that they had a boat, and ask him to send a message with the time and position for their meeting. Alina thought that dinnertime on a Friday at a Russian consulate may not be the best time to leave an important message. Tomorrow morning around ten o'clock would be much better. Alex laughed. He had not thought about the day and time. Of course, she was right. He had many rather foggy memories of Russian hospitality.

They got in the car and drove over to the hotel in the marina area. There were rooms available, so they checked in, dropped off their luggage, and walked over to a restaurant for dinner. This time, they both had a cocktail to celebrate their first dinner without jumping in the car right away. Alina was in high spirits.

"I really enjoyed hearing that I'm your fiancée now, even if it's just for fun," she said.

"Well," said Alex, "even if it's just for fun, we can still celebrate it, right?"

"I agree, but I am starving. Can we finish dinner first?"

Alex gave a big laugh. He had forgotten what he'd told himself a day or two ago—to be careful what he says to this lady.

Chapter 10

Linda was out of bed and ready for her morning exercise at 5:30. She had been dead tired when she went to bed at nine, but after eight hours of solid sleep, she felt both energetic and filled with anticipation for the day. After her workout and shower, she sat down and went through her file of the abducted children. The most recent kidnappings happened eleven and fifteen days ago, respectively, one in Cheyenne, Wyoming, and the most recent in Colorado Springs. Both were four-year-old blonde girls. Before that, the most recent were about three and four weeks ago, a five-year-old boy in Missoula, Montana, and a four-year-old boy in Seattle, Washington.

Linda was excited. She now knew, with close to certainty, who the parents of the two girls were. She also knew that the sooner the children were together with their parents, the faster their recovery would be. The next steps, however—how to get in touch with the presumed parents, knowing exactly what to say—she had no experience with. Hopefully someone in the group had some ideas.

She went down early to the group's seven o'clock breakfast to try and find a table for five in a somewhat private setting. That was not a problem. She got her breakfast, sat down, and enjoyed her coffee, yogurt, and boiled egg in quiet solitude. The others dropped in before she finished, all in high spirits after yesterday's events and the thought of sleeping in their own beds tonight. When all were seated and Linda had finished eating, she presented her dilemma.

"From my documentation about all the recent kidnappings, we now know with close to certainty that the two girls belong to a family in Cheyenne and a family in Colorado Springs, but we don't know which girl belongs to which family. The pictures I have are not clear enough to tell the girls apart. They look like twins. I need your help to come up with our next step: how to contact the families and what to say. This is a situation I have never been in or heard of. Anybody have any thoughts?"

The table was silent besides the rattling of coffee cups. After several minutes, Susan was the first to speak.

"There will be some time between the moment they are told that we have found two little girls and the moment they can see them and decide if they won or lost. We cannot avoid that. What we must do is make that time as short as possible. One way could be to take several pictures of the girls. Then we'll call the parents and tell them that we have found two girls, alive and well, and ask them to look at some pictures and see if they can identify them. To minimize time, we'll have a car just a block away with two agents—a man and a woman—and the pictures."

"Thank you, Susan," Linda said. "That could work. I like it. The two agents can take care of the logistics of bringing the parents here, at least from the Springs; it's only a three-hour drive. Cheyenne is closer to a five-hour drive; we'll probably use a plane for that. Comments, anybody?"

Steve liked the plan as well; it was practical and simple. The two remaining agents agreed, and Linda thanked them all. She had her plan, and it was time to get back to work.

Back at the compound, several sheriff's deputies were controlling traffic off the interstate and onto the bridge, keeping media people and curiosity seekers from crossing the crime scene barriers. Otherwise, the compound was empty and looked peaceful and beautiful.

Inside the white mansion, the lock crew had just started their second day, and the building was closed off. In the man cave were a few FBI agents, sheriff's deputies, and state troopers. There were also the pictures taken from the helicopter as they arrived the day before.

Linda sat down with her team of five agents. With the white mansion off-limits, their activities had been scaled back. She handed over the helicopter pictures to Susan to scrutinize and then turned to Steve.

"Steve, I will leave for the hospital and talk to Dr. Lopez. We need to get going with the girls. Can you take care of this place while I'm out? I want Bob to investigate the dirty deputy's communication, and we have a number of buildings here that have not been checked yet. The lock guys could be done at any time, hopefully today, and that might start the ball rolling again."

Steve said he was honored to be Linda's deputy, and in good spirits, the group started the day.

Linda asked Jeff Conner to join her. She called and asked for Dr. Lopez from the car. The doctor was busy but would be informed of their arrival. After the hospital, she planned to visit the yellow building where they had found the little girls again.

When Linda and Jeff entered the pediatric clinic, they were met by a smiling Dr. Lopez.

"Hi, Linda, I have good news," the doctor said. "The girls are recovering much quicker than I expected. They still need a lot of sleep, of course, but when they are awake, they are talking away with both each other and the nurses. The only thing missing is their families. If they were present, the girls could be discharged tomorrow."

"That is good news," Linda started. "We'll get in touch with the parents, hopefully tomorrow. To do that, we need to have some good pictures of the children to show to the parents. The pictures we have are not good enough; the girls look like they could be twins. Can the hospital arrange to get some new pictures taken where the girls look natural and smiling? We do not want to end up in a situation with uncertainty, or worst case, a mix-up."

Dr. Lopez's smile disappeared. "I didn't think about that. What a horrible situation for the parents. Yes, we'll make sure we get pictures of them without upsetting them. Actually, we'll make it fun for them." The doctor smiled again. "We should have them by the end of the day."

"Thank you so much. Could I see the girls at this point?"

"Yes, of course, they are used to different people walking in. They even seem to enjoy it. Everybody is so friendly and encouraging with them. I'll join you. You should put on some nurse garb so as not to confuse them."

As they walked through the room and looked at the little smiling girls, Linda's emotions were mixed. She was so happy to see them and so furious at the people who abducted them.

They left the hospital. Linda asked Jeff Conner to drive to the building where the girls had been found. She wanted to make sure that the officers on site looked for and saved any records of children who had passed through there. She was not in a good mood. She called Brian Thompson, who was the agent in charge, and let him know she was on her way.

Linda was met by Agent Thompson. He gave her Tanya's telephone, and then a quick briefing.

"The building has two parts. One is the nursery where the children were kept, and the other contains the living quarters and a room that seemed to be the office. We found financial records, a checkbook, and some cash in a desk. In the nursery, we found files with documents. There didn't seem to be any order or system, and it will take some time to sort through them all. What looked like the most recent documents, we put in a separate box. We also found boxes with drugs of different kinds stored in cabinets and closets. So far, we have not found any weapons or needles. There are several closets we haven't opened yet, and who knows what we may find. The time to finish the search, pack up everything, sanitize the place, and turn it over to the local government is more than a week with four people."

Linda thanked Agent Thompson for the briefing. She felt comfortable with their work and looked forward to any surprises they may discover.

On the way back, Steve called; the storage room was open and unarmed. That took care of a late lunch for Linda and Jeff.

The vault problem was also what had kept José's family away. She called José. "José, Agent Crawford here. I have some good news: You can bring your family back. I would also like you and María to take care of the food detail for all the officers on site. There are many people to feed around the clock. This work will be paid for by the FBI, so you have to set up a time sheet for both of you."

Linda was glad she had told him over the phone. That saved her from who knows how many hugs and kisses from this very emotional Colombian man.

Fifteen minutes later, Steve and Linda walked into the storage room. They could hardly believe their eyes. This was indeed a data center for an international corporation, with rows of processors and data storage devices. But *why*? None of them were enough of a data expert to dare to touch anything.

What they *could* understand, however, were several boxes at the end of the room. Some were filled with pills and powder in professionally marked and sealed plastic bags, and a few were filled with properly wrapped and marked bundles of dollar bills. Steve checked the weight of a couple of money boxes. They were heavy. They were looking at millions of dollars.

Linda called Tom from the mansion, which was now open again.

"Hi, Tom. We have some good news, finally. The lock guys got the door to the storage room, or rather vault, open without an explosion. It is something else . . . like the data center for the entire FBI. We don't dare to touch anything. Who knows what kind of destructive software is built in? We need a couple of guys who can break into this monster. Other things down here are drugs and money, lots of drugs and millions in cash. We need a truck to come and get that out of here as soon as it can be arranged."

"Well, congratulations. I'll get people and a truck up there tomorrow. It's too late today. And how does this affect your weekend off, as we talked about?"

"Oh yes, we all look forward to that. It's only a week away."

Tom chuckled, shaking his head. "I love you guys. Say hi to everyone for me."

"Will do," Linda said as she hung up.

She leaned back in the comfortable chair and tried to organize her thoughts. The highest priority now was the pictures of the little girls. They were about two hours away. Then she had the most pressing task: contacting the parents. She would have liked to do both visits herself, but that was not possible.

She set up a conference call with the FBI offices in Cheyenne and Colorado Springs. When she had both agents in charge on the line, she explained the reason for her call. They were both very familiar with all the shootings that had happened around Eagle County and had also heard about two young children who had been found. They would be honored to help and contact the parents to show them the pictures of the two little girls.

Linda went through the procedure she felt they should follow.

"My plan is to have a car with two agents, a woman and a man if possible. It should be done tomorrow, Saturday morning, around eleven, when most people are in their homes. If nobody answers, they should try to find their whereabouts from neighbors and relatives. They should show the pictures and tell the parents that the children are healthy and in the care of Dr. Sara Lopez at the pediatric clinic at Vail Hospital. They are ready to be picked up at any time. The FBI can arrange transportation and hotel accommodation in Vail close to the hospital if needed. The parents only must decide and let them know when they are ready to pick up their daughters. I will email the pictures, and I suggest they be printed for easier viewing in a very emotional situation."

When all was done, Linda drove over to the hospital. Exactly at four o'clock, she stepped out of her car at the pediatric clinic. Would they have useful pictures of the two girls? She found her way to Dr. Lopez's office. A nurse told her to go right in; Dr. Lopez was expecting her. She went in and was met by a relaxed doctor, who came up and hugged her.

"Linda, I'm so glad to see you. I can't tell you how much I admire your work, what you are doing for so many people hurt by those thugs. Come sit down." They walked over to a corner with a small table and two chairs, a modest but comfortable place to talk. On the table was a stack of pictures. "Here they are. Please take a look. We have them digitally as well, but I thought it would be easier to hand them over rather than pointing at them on a computer screen."

Linda went through the pictures. There were several double copies of each girl. The variety included everything from sad to shy to smiling. There was no doubt the parents would recognize their daughters.

"These are terrific," Linda said. "We'll try to show them to the parents tomorrow morning. We'll offer to take the parents here and put them up in a hotel until their child can be discharged, and then take them back home. I'm both excited and a bit scared that we've mixed up some names. There's always an element of uncertainty in this job."

"I guess we're all dealing with uncertainties, whatever our jobs are. When you are done, Linda, please call me and let me know what happens, whether it's good or bad. I'm so emotionally stirred up by this whole thing, and I'm not supposed to be in my job. Here's my card and number. Call me day or night. And when this is behind us, I want to see you and your husband at our home someday. I think we have a lot to talk about. The guys can sit somewhere and talk about their football and fishing."

"Thank you, Sara, I would enjoy that. And thanks for taking such good care of the girls. I'll talk to you tomorrow."

Linda left with two envelopes and very strong feelings of both hope and hopelessness—hope for these two girls and hopelessness for five other young children who may never see their parents again.

She walked through the hospital to see Dr. Black and Tanya. The doctor was in surgery, a nurse said, but Linda was welcome to visit Tanya.

Tanya was very happy to see Linda again and get her phone back. It had only been a day since they last met, but sitting alone in a hospital room with guards outside while not being sick would take its toll on anybody. Linda suggested Tanya call her cousin right away. They had still no idea where she was. Tanya called but got no answer. She looked very worried.

"Tanya, I don't think you need to be worried about Alina," Linda said. "From all that's happened, we know that she's fine and not alone. We believe she is in the company of one or more insiders who found out that the business they worked for was a front for something very different and very bad. That organization has now been taken down with the shootings two days ago, but nobody knows if there are some members still around. Both you and Alina have to be protected. What I'm telling you here is highly confidential. You can only talk about it with FBI agents, but it's important that you know so you understand your own situation with guards, confidentiality, and discomfort."

Tanya was listening and slowly shaking her head.

"Alina must have picked up on this before I did," she said. "Now I understand why they kept giving us those drugs. Alina didn't take any. She sometimes pretended to be obedient, but she never took anything. But what happens to Alina and me now when those people are dead? I guess we have to go back home to Russia."

"It's way too early to decide anything, but our first priority is your safety. My advice to you is to put up with all our restrictions to be sure that you'll be safe when it's over. And of course, work with the doctor to get off the drug dependence they got you in."

Linda got up, ready to leave. Tanya got up as well and gave Linda a big hug.

"Thank you so much," Tanya said. "I'm so thankful for everything you have done. I think we all knew something was terribly wrong, but maybe we were just too drugged to react. I hope to see you again soon."

Linda left and drove back to the compound. It was close to six, and the day was almost over. She met with Steve, who informed her that two hackers would join them in the morning. That was good news. Maybe tomorrow would bring them some badly needed information.

Chapter 11

Alex and Alina woke up the next morning around eight, still tired and very happy. They had long showers and a slow breakfast before they were ready to check out. It was close to ten—the right time for Alina to make her call. Her uncle answered after a few rings, and Alina talked with him for several minutes in Russian. After the call, she told Alex that her uncle was glad to hear from her but sounded tired. He promised to get back to her with a specific meeting time and coordinates in about a week. He said he looked forward to seeing her; it had been almost ten years since they last saw each other.

Alex and Alina checked out and went to the nearest shopping mall. The weather was good for Seattle on this last day of March, around sixty degrees and overcast but not rainy. Their shopping list was not too exhausting: a contract form, a bottle of champagne, two money envelopes, and a wedding card for the two young Danes. As they were driving back to the marina, Alex turned toward Alina.

"Just as a reminder for both of us," he said, "to them, I am Mark Walker, and the boat will be in your name. We live in Denver, Colorado, and we're planning to sail north to Alaska this summer."

"I love that plan, to sail to Alaska with my new friend Mark. I hope he's as nice as my old friend Alex," she said as she bent over and kissed his cheek. Alex shook his head.

At noon, they were back at the marina for a tour of what would soon be their new boat. On the dock were a number of boxes and a few duffel bags. Jorgen stepped onto the dock and greeted them. He pointed at the boxes and said that they included all their bedding, bathroom stuff, and food. They had left behind foul-weather clothing since they thought their sizes would fit them. They also left binoculars, all their navigation and boat literature, and tools, as well as kitchen utensils.

They stepped on board and met Lisa, who greeted them with her contagious smile. She said she would stay in the cockpit since four people moving around downstairs would be a crowd.

They started the tour down in the cabin. Jorgen pointed out the bunks, the galley, the head, and the navigation station. He lifted the companionway stairs and showed them the diesel engine. In the cockpit, he started with the sprayhood, which could be totally folded down, raised to function as a fair-weather sprayhood, or extended to a foul-weather cover. He went through the various control functions and the wind vane, the wind-powered autopilot. He made the point that the wind vane steered the boat only when they were under sail, of course. There was also a compass, a plotter, a VHF, and engine controls.

Finally, he pointed to the rubber dinghy in front of the mast and the three-horsepower outboard engine hanging on the transom railing. It was a quick introduction. Jorgen asked "Mark" how he wanted to proceed with his inspection. "Mark" explained that he wanted to check all the functions and then take her out on a test sail.

It was close to six o'clock when it was all done, and Alex could tell Jorgen that he was indeed a man of his word. Everything worked perfectly on this sixty-year-old beauty. Alina agreed and added that they were ready to close the transaction.

Alex dug around in a shopping bag he had brought and took out the contract. They had already filled in all the numbers, dates, and Alina's name. Jorgen filled in the sellers' names and the boat's serial number. He was the title holder, so the transaction was between him and Alina. When it was signed, Alina took out an envelope from the shopping bag and handed it to Jorgen. After he counted the money, she took out another envelope and handed it to Lisa. After the money in the second envelope was counted, Alina took out the bottle of champagne and the wedding card. Alex was watching the whole procedure with a smile on his face.

"Great! Let's celebrate the deal," Jorgen said and reached for the champagne.

"I don't think that's a good idea," Alina protested. "Both of you have worked so hard getting the boat cleaned and ready that the only celebration you need right now is a good dinner and an early evening, just the two of you."

Lisa, who had not said a word in the last hour, got up and hugged Alina. "Thank you so much, Alina. I am dead tired. All I can take now is a little salad and then sleep."

"But where are you going to sleep?" Alina asked. "Why don't you sleep here tonight and leave tomorrow at noon? We have to buy all the sheets, pillows, and towels anyway. The boat will be empty tonight, and I don't like that at all."

"Please, darling, let's do that," Lisa pleaded with Jorgen.

"Of course," Jorgen said, "but you were so happy to find a hotel room earlier. I would like to stay too if we can do that."

Alina agreed. She and Alex said good night and went up to the dock. There, Alex gave Jorgen a hand in putting all the boxes and bags back on board. They waved good night and walked back to the car. Hopefully, they would be able to stay at the same hotel for another night.

"What was all that about?" Alex asked. "You didn't want to stay on your new boat suddenly?"

"Men are so blind. Didn't you see—Lisa is pregnant? And she worked all day getting the boat ready . . . I hope by God she will be OK." Alex said nothing, just shook his head.

They got a room at the same hotel, went to the same restaurant, and had the same cocktails. But that was enough. The dinners they ordered were different. After dinner, they walked back to the hotel holding hands. It had been a good day for both. Like springtime in their relationship. They treasured the moment.

Chapter 12

The two computer specialists, or hackers, as Steve called them, arrived by plane at 10:30 Saturday morning and took an Uber to the compound. They certainly were an odd couple. Ian was a clean-cut, fortyish, somewhat round man with mild manners who wore a shirt and tie, jacket, coat, hat, and slacks. Nick was much younger. He looked about nineteen but was probably in his mid-twenties. He had long, unkempt hair and was unshaven. He wore jeans, sneakers, and an old, well-worn, brown leather jacket. Both men carried a heavy briefcase and a carry-on. This could take many days.

Linda and Steve met them, and they all walked to the conference room. Linda introduced herself and Steve and gave a short summary of the background to the hackers' visit. Nick whistled when he heard about the shootings and uttered some very strong words when he heard about the kidnappings. Ian was mute.

Steve talked about the computer room, which they would soon visit. He told them about the lock and his suspicions that this room held information about the organization's illegal activities over several years, including drug smuggling, trafficking, and kidnappings, all potentially with international connections. It was imperative that nothing was lost as they started to dig into the system. One of the most important elements was to find any international connections with whom the organization had been in contact and done business. Steve mentioned this in case it was easier to find addresses than content. Neither hacker commented.

They walked down to the storage room. Even Ian let out some sound of surprise and muttered something about modern-day aircraft carriers. Nick looked like a kid in a candy store. His eyes twinkled as he walked around and took in the beauty of all the processors and storage units.

After the visit, they were again in the conference room. Steve asked Ian and Nick about their background and experience. Nobody said anything for a while. Nick was the first to speak.

"We have worked together for around six years. Ian was my mentor and still is in many situations. People tell us we are good. I don't know; there is no rating in this field. We work mostly for the military. They have a lot of self-sustained systems just like this one. My first reaction was that this was put in by some military contractor. It looks familiar, and if it is, we should be able to get some readings in a day or so. It will take us an hour to determine the nature of this beauty."

Ian was silent. Then he suddenly spoke. "Let's go."

They took their heavy bags and went down again. Steve and Linda looked at each other and couldn't help smiling. Maybe this was the beginning of the end of this whole project.

Two hours later, in time for a late lunch, Ian and Nick came back up. Linda happened to be in the command center finishing the second call from the agents in Cheyenne and Colorado Springs. Both families had been reached and the children had been identified. Both were now driving to Vail to pick up their daughters. The Colorado Springs parents should arrive around 2:00 p.m. and the Cheyenne parents around 4:00 p.m.

She called Steve, who was outside talking with some officers, and told him the good news. She then asked him to join her for a report from the data center. She also called María regarding lunch and was told that a lunch buffet was set up in the man cave. María would make sure that the coffee was fresh.

When Steve arrived, Nick started to talk.

"The entire installation is similar to what the military is using. There are three contractors who are qualified and share the business. This installation has a few variations, but we're certain it's been built by one of them. There's nothing illegal about it; there are no proprietary components or subsystems that we've seen so far. We have a list of all communication addresses from this year, but getting to the content will take a while. One of the addresses in Canada has repeatedly tried to contact them over the last few days."

"Thank you," Steve said. "Is the address list ready to be looked at right now, or is it in some code?"

"We can print it out now, but it would only contain addresses from the last three months," Nick answered.

"Please do that, and then try to get the list for last year. I think that will tell us if we need to go back another year," Steve finished.

Ian and Nick walked down to their vault. They both came back up after about fifteen minutes with the list for the last three months. Nick pointed out that the contact in Canada who tried to get in touch over the last few days seemed to have stopped their effort earlier this morning. The address was the Russian consulate in Vancouver.

Nick looked at Linda when he said this. He had expected some kind of reaction after what they had been told, and he was not disappointed. She sank down into her chair. All the blood seemed to leave her face, and her eyes stared straight out.

"This is absolutely secret. You cannot talk about this with anybody—not *anybody*. Steve, you remember what Tom said two weeks ago, that it looked like Russia or China? Now we know it's Russia. The whole damned country of Russia is here stealing our children. Through their embassy!" Linda said with a display of anger Steve had never seen before.

Nobody said a word for a long while. Linda broke the silence. "Let's have something to eat, if that is possible right now. Then Steve, you and I have to call Tom and ruin his weekend."

With that, she stood up and walked with the others over to the man cave where María had arranged lunch. The other officers had already finished eating, so they had the place to themselves.

As soon as they entered, María came over and hugged both Linda and Steve and thanked them so much for allowing her back and having something to do here.

All four got some food and sat down to eat. Nobody spoke. Steve broke the silence.

"OK, guys, this is both good and bad news, and that comes with the territory. Let's enjoy the food. That will help us cope with whatever we are dealt."

With that, he started to get into his lunch, and the others slowly caught up.

When lunch was finished, Ian and Nick headed back to their vault, and Steve and Linda went to the office to call Tom. Steve insisted that Linda make the call and talk to him.

"Good afternoon," Tom answered. "I take it you have some exciting news to interrupt my favorite Saturday sports show."

"Yes, sir, we do. Are you sitting down right now?" Linda asked.

"I just sat down. Shoot."

"The most recent and active address in the system here is the Russian consulate in Vancouver, Canada. At this point, we just have the addresses. Sometime tomorrow, we will also have content."

There was a silent moment before Tom spoke.

"I'll be damned! You call me whenever the content is known. This is enough to alert the president, but it would be good to have some specifics. My goodness, Linda, you really set some balls in motion. And this was the weekend I was giving you guys off to be home with your families. I'm glad you turned it down."

"Another question, Tom. I think this gives us reason to check with the RCMP if they have had any kidnappings like these in Canada. Who handles that, you or me?"

"I know a Mountie captain in Vancouver. I'll take care of it. Thank you, Linda."

Linda told Steve it was time for her to drive over to the hospital and release the girls. The parents from Colorado Springs could arrive any minute now. The Cheyenne parents were probably a couple of hours away. She got one of the Steamboat agents, Jeff Conner, to drive. She was too upset to drive safely.

At the hospital, Linda asked if Dr. Lopez was around this Saturday afternoon. The nurse said she was not but that she was on call for when Agent Crawford or the parents showed up. The nurse made the call and then told Linda that Dr. Lopez would soon join her.

When Dr. Lopez arrived, she told the nurse that she would be in her office and should be notified when the parents arrived. The entire hospital was emotionally involved in this case. Every doctor, nurse, staff member, and patient wanted to see a glimpse of both the parents and the little girls. So did the media, of course, but the hospital was not giving out any information. The parents would have private reunions with their daughters—doctor's orders.

Dr. Lopez took Linda back to her office. They sat down in her little social corner. Her first question was how Linda's investigation was going.

"Oh gosh, Sara, I was hoping you wouldn't ask. It's all classified. But I can say that we had a break only about an hour ago. We know who is behind this, and it's not good. I don't know when I can sleep again, and please don't ask me for more information. I only told you this so you can understand if I seem erratic or distraught, it's because I am."

They both sat silent for some moments. Then Sara said, "I won't ask you anything except how you are doing. I may be a pediatric doctor, but that doesn't mean I can't help grown-ups as well. You know, size is the only difference, and size doesn't matter. We know that." Linda laughed, and Sara joined her.

"Thank you, Sara. You have already helped me. And I may take you up on your offer. If I feel down, I'll call you. You know more about what's going on here than anybody else, including my husband, Mark."

"Speaking of Mark, you're up here full time, right?" Sara asked.

"Yes, but so far, it's only been since Wednesday. Three days, although it seems like three weeks. I was thinking of asking Mark to come up this weekend, but our investigation is in a very intense phase. I may not see him even if he's here."

"I understand," Sara said. "You work, eat, and sleep as a group, like we do here when it gets crazy."

"Exactly. Healthcare and first responders have that in common. Bad things don't run on a nine-to-five schedule."

Sara's phone rang. The parents from Colorado Springs had arrived. Linda and Sara both got up and walked out to the lobby. They met the parents and their son, Charlie. They all walked into an examination room, where Sara introduced herself and FBI agent Linda Crawford. The father asked Agent Crawford what she could tell about the whole kidnapping story. Linda was prepared to say as little as possible.

"It was a very fortunate event. A woman working at a nursery here in Eagle got suspicious about two girls who came into the nursery. Their parents had died, but they were not sisters. Two four-year-old girls had both lost their parents at about the same time, and nobody had heard about any accident. She contacted the police, and that's how this was cleared up," Linda explained.

"Wow, what a stroke of luck. If they had been a year apart ..." He did not finish his sentence. A nurse walked in with his daughter.

Sara, Linda, and the nurse left the room after telling them they would wait outside. After about ten minutes, the door opened, and the family stepped out. They were happy. The father asked how this would be handled paperwork-wise.

"Up until now, your daughter Tina has been in custody of the FBI," Linda answered. "To release her, we'll need both parents' IDs and signatures on this release document. Let's go back into the room, where we can sit down and go over it."

The two siblings were fully occupied with each other. When all the paperwork was finished, Linda left the room to let the doctor go over Tina's medical issues with the parents. Linda would wait outside. When they all came back out, the parents hugged and thanked Linda before they left for home.

When they were gone, Linda turned to Sara and said, "I don't know if I can take more of this roller coaster. Total disaster one minute and complete happiness the next. Do you have any pills for that?"

They both laughed as they walked back to Sara's office. It was three o'clock, and the next family would arrive in an hour or so.

In the office, Linda excused herself. She needed to call her deputy, Steve, who was her boss back at the office. Sara looked puzzled but said nothing.

Steve had no news. He had recently visited the hackers, who told him they were making progress but did not believe they would have any content until the following day.

The Cheyenne couple arrived about forty minutes later. They went through the same routine, and again the father asked about the kidnapping, how it had happened, and how his daughter had been found. Linda told the same story about how the girls had been found that she had told the other father. How the kidnapping had happened was still under investigation.

*   *   *

Linda woke up late on Sunday morning. It was 7:30, a gray day with snow in the air. She started the day with a hot shower and skipped her exercise routine; it was too late for that. She made herself a cup of coffee and then called Mark. They had not had a good conversation since she had left on Wednesday. That was in late March, and now it was April. A whole month between calls, Mark would say.

It was relaxing to talk to Mark, her husband and best friend. She covered the many surprises and discoveries the few days had brought, although she could not share the biggest of them all: the Russian connection. The call lasted almost an hour, and she felt a lot better when she hung up—like a load had been taken off her back.

Then she called Steve to coordinate their day. He picked up on the first ring.

"Hey, are you OK? I was starting to worry."

"Yes, I am fine, better than I can remember. I think we have had some very productive days, and now I am anxious to hear what our hacker friends have discovered. Any news yet?"

"Not yet. And what about you? Do you need a ride? I can send Jeff over."

"Thanks, Steve. That would be perfect. See you in a bit."

When they got back to the estate, Linda wanted to hear from the officers who had been searching the many outbuildings. Two FBI agents came in and gave their reports. There was a lot of farm equipment, a couple of tractors, a tool room, and a shed with lumber. There was also a room with a concrete floor and drainage, hoists, and cutting tools—a big-game butcher room. Nothing was suspicious or illegal so far. They were down to the last couple of rather small buildings and should be done by the end of the day, barring any surprises.

Ian and Nick came up just before noon. Linda and Steve were still in the command center, and they all sat down around the table.

"We have printed out some content," Nick started, "but so far, only from the Russian connection. We thought you would be interested, like right away. We will print it all later."

He pushed over a few pages toward Linda. She picked them up. There were six letters, one on each page, between the Russian consulate and the white mansion. There were no names.

Linda read one page at a time and then handed it over to Steve. When they were both done reading, she thanked the hackers and said, "This is all the proof we need about Russia's involvement, but we need everything you guys can find to help track the other missing children. Good luck on the hunt, and Steve, it's time to get Tom involved."

She scanned the pages and emailed them to Tom. She included an "urgent" beep and waited a minute before calling him. Tom picked up right away.

"Thank you," he started. "This is what we need. I will call the director right away. It's his job to deal with POTUS. But be prepared, he will probably call you when I run out of answers to his hundred questions. Thanks again, Linda. Your name will be on POTUS's desk tomorrow morning, and you know what that means?"

"Well, maybe I'll get dinner at the real White House," Linda laughed.

"That's probably a safe guess. And also, Linda, a mail just came in from my Mounty friend. They have had four similar abductions in the western provinces. The spread in geography and time had kept them under the radar so far. You are on their fan list as well. Thanks again, Linda, and goodbye."

Steve, who had overheard the conversation, congratulated Linda and suggested they break for lunch. She agreed and they walked over to the man cave.

There was not much of a buzz around the tables. What happened inside the white mansion was not known to anybody there, and the search jobs brought no excitement. Linda told the sheriff's deputies that all she needed for the rest of the weekend was Deputy Darby's traffic and security group. The little that remained of the search job could be handled by Jeff and Roger. They had agreed that they could finish the search before the end of the day unless something unexpected came up. The only other job they could be involved in was the security detail keeping Tanya safe at the hospital.

Linda and Steve walked over to the owner's office. It was a very comfortable place to sit and talk.

"What do you think will happen now?" Linda asked. "The involvement of an embassy in an extremely serious criminal activity against the people in the host country is new to me. In my view, it's an act of war. Of course, the embassy in this case is in Canada, not the US, but that technicality can hardly change the picture much."

Steve was quiet for a long time. Then he simply said, "I agree. It's an act of war. And on that upbeat note, let's call it a day with a glass of good port from this extensive bar."

Linda agreed. They still had to hang around and lock up the house when Ian and Nick were done.

Less than an hour later, Linda's phone rang. It was Aaron Wrangler, the Director of the FBI and one of the most powerful men in DC. At least under J. Edgar Hoover's rule.

The director started by congratulating Linda for making a breakthrough in this incredible crime mystery. She thanked him and pointed out that there were several people involved, including the sheriff's office, state troopers, and many other FBI agents.

"OK, Linda, I know all that, but I also know quite a bit about this whole story. You can't escape a large part of the credit here. But the one thing I couldn't fully grasp was the part about the two Russian cousins, why they were there and what they did. Can you tell me about their involvement again?

"I can tell you what I have been told," Linda said. "Tanya is thirty-three years old. She has been here for almost two years working for this not-for-profit organization. Good pay, not much work. She convinced her cousin Alina to join her. Alina was a teacher in Russia and had just been through a divorce. She is about forty-three, and she's also a skier. She came over to America for a break and to ski.

"The organization pushed the girls to use drugs, starting with opioids before transitioning them to heavier stuff. We don't know why—possibly to dull their instincts and suspicions. Alina did not take anything and was treated as an outsider. Her time to ski was taken away, and she got more and more unhappy. Two supervisors made sure she did not leave. Then she disappeared during the night a few hours before the shooting at the estate, which happened at noon last Wednesday. Mid-morning the next day, she called Tanya, gave her my number, and told her to call me.

"Tanya called me and told me her location. She said she had found two sleeping children in a room. We took the helicopter and called for ambulances and a pediatric doctor. The two small children were unconscious, and the doctor took care of them. Then, Tanya told us about another place. We flew there and found three bodies, no survivors, and a bag sitting on the kitchen counter with about $150,000. Two of the bodies were the supervisors who had watched Alina and the other girls; the third body was a female caretaker. That's what I know."

It took a while before the director spoke. "That's quite a story. Looking at all those incidents, we have to assume that Alina is involved in the shootings, although we don't know how. It sounds like she hooked up with somebody who knows something about the FBI and has a shotgun. Not necessarily a professional shooter; it doesn't take much skill to use a shotgun. What do you think?"

"We have talked about this, of course. We do not believe it's an insider. The only shooters in the organization, according to Tanya, were the two guys who were killed. It's more likely that Alina came to know a hunter or law enforcement officer, and the two of them were upset enough to take down the whole operation."

"Good. That sounds plausible. Now, the most important question: How solid are the links to Russia? Give me every piece of evidence."

"We have correspondence between the computer system here and the Russian consulate in Vancouver, Canada. It includes detailed descriptions of 'items' to be delivered, like a four-year-old female with blue eyes, blonde hair, and a normal size and shape. The correspondence also includes the delivery methods, like a fishing boat out of Portland, Oregon, meeting up with a Russian fishing boat at specific coordinates and times. We have a couple of those, and our hacker team is right now digging back in time to find more. I should also mention that the 'item' I just described, and another girl, were saved by Tanya and returned to their families yesterday."

The director spoke slowly. "I have never heard anything like this before. It's both infuriating and touching. I have no idea what the President's reaction will be when I talk to him tomorrow, but be prepared—he may want to hear from you directly just as I did. Now my last question: How did you find all this? In the computer?"

"Yes. There is a storage room here in the basement. The lock required both a code and face recognition, which raised our curiosity. We brought a couple of experts up. They got us in after about a day's work. There were no explosives. Then we got a couple of hackers, who have been here for two days now.

"The hackers got an address list after a couple of hours, and the Russian consulate in Vancouver was the most frequent and most recent contact. They had made several attempts to get in touch after the shootings. A day later, the hackers got the content of the last few correspondences. They included the descriptions of the 'items,' among other things. We also found large stacks of money in the storage room—several million just by the look of it—and crates with drugs."

Linda felt emotionally exhausted after rehashing all that happened in the last several days. Luckily, Director Wrangler had no more questions. He thanked Linda and said he was going to practice his presentation to the President with a call to his Canadian counterpart, the Commissioner of the Royal Canadian Mounted Police.

Steve had been in the room with Linda through the call. He congratulated her on a brilliant summary of a very messy story and handed her another glass of port, this one well-filled. She thanked him and took the glass without protest. Their workday was over.

The hackers surfaced about half an hour later. They had printed hundreds of pages from the last three months. Tomorrow they would start on the previous year's correspondence.

They all got up to leave for the hotel. Steve drove. Nobody spoke. None of them would forget this Sunday.

Chapter 13

Alex and Alina woke up with the sun shining in the room. That was normal; the rest was not. They were tangled together in one big heap of arms, legs, hands, and feet. Some of their limbs were still asleep. Neither of them could find a free hand or foot to start and untangle the mess. After a few minutes, they were free and lying on the bed side by side, breathing hard and laughing. Alina rolled over to give Alex a hug.

"Hold it!" he cautioned. "You don't want to tie that knot again."

"Yes, I do," Alina said with a big smile, and Alex once more had to remind himself to think twice before saying anything.

They got up to start the new day. They would eat breakfast and then shop for everything they would need on the boat.

Alex had set up some parameters. They would sail out to meet Alina's uncle Igor. The first step was to sail to Neah Bay, which was about 120 miles away. That would take four days or so, depending on the weather and their stamina. There they would wait for the message from Alina's uncle with the time and position for their meeting, which could only take place in calm weather.

After that, they would sail north to Ketchikan, Alaska, about seven hundred miles away. Alex estimated that the time to get there would be about a month, depending on the weather, so they needed to buy food and water for five weeks. If their trip took longer, he could always take the dinghy to some Canadian town and get more provisions. If he was checked and asked for his passport, he would show his driver's license and claim emergency.

Alina wrote a list of what she could think of buying, and Alex crossed out what they didn't need. They had foul-weather clothing on board, so they only needed some bed sheets, blankets, pillows, towels, and enough food for five weeks. Well, Alina decided that she needed a few other things: salt-water shampoo, sunscreen, a bathing suit, sweaters, a warm jacket, boat shoes, gloves, and so on. Alex reminded her that it was early April, and they were in Washington State. The water was always cold, and the sky was always cloudy—well, mostly. They found a compromise without any lengthy discussion. Alina got what she wanted. It was paid for by the bad guys, so why not?

They went on their shopping spree. Everything on the list was found at an REI, a West Marine, a bedding store, and a supermarket. The whole expedition took about four hours.

Back at the marina, they off-loaded their shopping bags onto a couple of luggage carts. Jorgen and Lisa were waiting to finalize the deal. All their belongings had already been moved to the hotel. After some farewell wishes and hugs, the Danish couple left for home and a new and very different life.

About an hour later, all their luggage was on board and in place. Alex had decided to drive the pickup to the long-term parking at the airport and come back in an Uber. There was little chance anybody would know who had put the pickup there, and if they or he came back in the next couple of weeks, the car could still be there. If they went to Alaska, they could forget about the car; that trip would take at least three months.

Alex drove the car to the airport and returned two hours later. When he went down into the cabin, he sat down with a big smile. Alina had cleaned up and decorated the little salon so that it looked very inviting and comfortable. Alex gave her a big hug.

"Thank you for making it look so nice," he said. "Now we have our own place and can just relax, eat a little, drink some wine, make love, and not worry about a thing. What do you say, sweetheart?"

"I say yes, Captain. Isn't that what I'm supposed to say?"

"Always," he said as he handed her a glass of wine.

They woke up at daybreak. Alex went up to the cockpit to check things out. It was a nice morning, overcast and cool with a northerly breeze, somewhere around five knots. It would be a good day to get to know the boat and introduce Alina to sailing; it was her first time on a sailboat.

They had a quick breakfast of coffee and sandwiches and decided to get going right away. Alex started the engine and turned on the instruments. He showed Alina the plotter and how it worked. Then he disconnected the lines, rolled them up, and stowed them, all the time making sure Alina saw what he did and understood why.

Once untied, he maneuvered the boat between the docks out on open water. Besides the short test sail, it was his first experience with a tiller, and it surprised him how easy it was to use. It was more direct, and he had a better feel for handling the boat. He found a comfortable speed at four knots and handed the tiller to Alina. She was excited about the whole situation and enjoyed being in control.

On the plotter, Alex picked an island about forty miles away, which would be their first overnight anchoring spot. The journey had begun. He showed Alina their position, the anchoring island, and the route they had to follow to get there. He also explained the markers they could see and some basic rules of the sea.

The wind was barely strong enough to move the boat, so Alex decided to keep the engine running and wait to set sail until the wind picked up. It was a nice day, with *Springtime* leisurely cruising through the modest waves on the protected waters of Puget Sound. They were dressed for early April on the water with sweaters, windbreakers, and warm hats. The extended sprayhood was up. Alina's smile was permanent.

Alex made lunch: sandwiches, coffee, fruit, and chocolate truffles for dessert. Alina gave him a big hug and a kiss, and the boat took an unplanned turn. She quickly corrected the situation and looked surprised over the boat's reaction.

Alex laughed, "Boats are females, and you made *Springtime* jealous with your display of affection for me."

"I'm so sorry! I didn't know that, and I promise not to do it again, at least not out in the open. I hope this lady doesn't have eyes in the salon, or we'll be in great trouble. And I won't let go of the tiller in case that had something to do with her reaction as well."

At around two o'clock, Alina's phone buzzed. It was a message from her uncle. She read it and looked at Alex with a puzzled face. Her uncle wrote that they had to leave earlier than planned—on Wednesday this week. Would she be able to meet up that soon? It was only two days away. Alex thought for a while.

"We can do that if we go nonstop," he said. "You steer when I sleep and vice versa. It's not as bad as it sounds. We will be in protected water all night in the Strait of Juan de Fuca. Our only concern is to keep clear of Vancouver Island to the north, the US to the south, and islands, markers, and other vessels, of course. We will be in Neah Bay this time tomorrow. We'll sleep there and buy fuel. Then we'll leave on Wednesday morning to meet your uncle. It's up to you, pretty girl."

"I can do it," Alina said after some thinking. She sent a response to her uncle.

They were silent for a few minutes, just gliding through the water, listening to the engine humming and the seagulls screaming. There were few boats out, mainly just fishing boats, some ferries, and a couple of merchant ships. Otherwise, the only sound disturbing the peace were jets coming and going from Seattle's international airport and Boeing's huge plant. The leisure boating season was still a month away.

An hour later, Uncle Igor responded. He looked forward to seeing Alina very much. She would get a message with their meeting time and position on Wednesday morning.

"OK, this will work fine," Alex said. "We'll just cruise along, eat, and sleep for twenty-four hours. This is what sailing is all about. Except we are not sailing; we are motorboating."

Alina smiled. After a while, she said, "I love this. It's peaceful and beautiful, and I'm with you. We've been together for five days now, and I've never felt like this: safe, comfortable, and totally happy. I wish it would never change."

Alex felt the same way. When he lost his wife, the first and only woman he had ever loved, he was content to spend the rest of his life by himself. His family, friends, and hobbies were all he needed. And now this Russian woman had entered his organized life and thrown everything into chaos. She was twenty years his junior, and after only five crazy days together, he knew that a life with her would be a gamble. He also knew he had to roll the dice.

"Alina, I want to see your smile every day for the rest of my life."

Alina came over and just kissed his cheek. Anything else would have thrown the boat off course.

At dinnertime, they ate and brought some warm blankets into the cockpit. The sun was dropping, and with it, so was the temperature. Alex turned on the navigation lights, explained them to Alina, and continued, "Why don't you take the helm for the next few hours, until ten o'clock? Stay this course and make sure the boat is about an inch from land on the plotter. That's about one mile. I'll sleep up here so all you have to do is shout "Captain" if something bothers you."

"Yes, Captain!" she responded immediately and smiled.

Alex tucked in under a warm cover and was asleep in a minute.

*   *   *

He woke up with a jump. Alina smiled at him.

"Good morning, Captain. I hope you slept well."

Alex checked the time. It was past three in the morning.

"My goodness, I slept through my whole watch. You should have woken me up at ten. What happened?"

Alina smiled. "I tried but you didn't respond. You must have been very tired."

Alex just shook his head and, after some moments, said, "Why don't you get a sandwich and then go to bed down in the cabin?"

"That's not a good idea. This place must be very comfortable; I couldn't even wake you up. I'll sleep here."

When Alina got to sleep, Alex tried to get a grip of the rendezvous they were heading into. Red flags were flying, and he had not shared them with Alina.

First, Uncle Igor was a diplomat. Although accredited to Canada and not the US, he knew the laws better than most. So why on earth did they have to meet thirty miles out when international waters start twelve miles offshore? Then, his vessel would travel the same route they were going. They could have stopped anywhere to talk, one vessel to another. Even if Alina did board Uncle Igor's vessel, nothing illegal would happen as long as she didn't step ashore in Canada.

And all these departure changes? And a seventy-plus-year-old, high-level diplomat taking a fishing boat to Russia for his retirement as a means of transportation, not for fishing? And inviting his niece on that ridiculous journey?

It all had a rotten smell, and it wasn't from old fish. One thing was clear—Alex would have his gun loaded, and Alina could not be aware of it.

Jorgen had told Alex that the wind vane, the wind-powered autopilot, only worked under sail. Instead of trying to prove him wrong, Alex took a couple of lines and rigged them around the tiller and some cleats until he had a contraption that only needed occasional adjustments to keep the boat on course. Smooth water was of course a requirement.

Alina was deep asleep. He caught himself smiling as he looked at the bundle she was part of. *So smart. So fun. So beautiful.* Would he suddenly wake up from a dream in his bed back home? He leaned back and enjoyed the quiet night.

The rising sun looked like it was lighting fire to the pine trees along the strait. It was just past seven in the morning, and there was only an hour or two left of their first leg to Neah Bay. They would go in, drop anchor, and maybe get a couple of hours of sleep. The night passage had been a lot easier than Alex had anticipated. But of course, Alina had taken the brunt of the work. What was he going to do with her? Or more to the point, *without* her?

Alina woke up around eight just as they approached the bay. She was totally amazed at the beauty of the morning with the sun rising above the snow-covered peak of Mount Olympus. They dropped anchor around nine o'clock and ate breakfast in the most beautiful place on Earth, according to Alina.

Chapter 14

Director Wrangler placed the call at 8:50 a.m. That would give the switchboard and the secretary time to hand the telephone to the president at 9:00 a.m. sharp. The president was high on punctuality, which also meant that the call would be over in exactly five minutes, including greetings and courtesy phrases.

"Good morning, Aaron. How was your weekend?" the president opened.

"Good morning, Mr. President. May I answer that question after my report, sir?" the director responded.

"Well, that certainly piqued my curiosity. What's going on?"

"Mr. President, yesterday the FBI got full proof that Russia is behind several kidnappings in the northwestern states of the US and the western provinces of Canada. Russia has been using its consulate in Vancouver as a transfer point for bringing children out of the US and Canada to a third country, presumably itself.

"Over the last five months, seven American and four Canadian children, all between four and five years old, have been abducted and, presumably, sent to Russia. The entire plot started to unravel last Wednesday. We got indications of Russia's role on Saturday and full proof yesterday. One piece of good news is that two of the abducted children were found on Thursday and, after medical treatment, are now back with their parents. That's my report, sir."

There was a long pause before the president spoke. "I am greatly disturbed, Aaron. I know you well enough to know what you say is true. Russia is using its Vancouver consulate, part of its Canadian embassy, to siphon off our children. This is war, damn it. To start, all this falls under the highest security. Not a word out. Is it too late for that?"

"That has been done, sir."

"Good. Come over for lunch with a few guys. Thanks, Aaron."

The president told his chief of staff to invite the secretaries of defense, state, and homeland security to join him for a private lunch together with the director of the FBI. The president then called the Canadian prime minister.

"Good morning, Pierre, I have just been informed that Russia is involved in a systematic activity of stealing children from the US and Canada through their consulate in Vancouver. Have you been briefed about that?" the president asked.

"Yes, I was briefed this morning, and I am furious. As far as I know, it's the first time in history a country has used its diplomatic establishment to harm the people in the host country. I consider this an act of war!" the prime minister declared.

"I see it the same way. The US has been attacked as well. I suggest we make a joint response for stronger impact. We need to meet as soon as possible and decide the course of action. Would you accept a meeting at Camp David, away from the public eye, in the next few days?"

"I appreciate the invitation. To me, this is the most serious crisis of my lifetime. I will be available any day, the sooner the better."

"Good. Let's meet tomorrow then, starting with lunch. Thanks, Pierre."

*   *   *

The activity in the White House over the following twenty-four hours was at a level rarely seen. Secrecy was at the highest level, and the political pundits, who smelled juicy news at the slightest variation in the White House routines, cringed over the lack of information.

The president opened the lunch meeting by asking the director of the FBI to repeat his report. It took Director Wrangler less than two minutes to read the report again. It was dead silent when he finished.

"Can you give the background to this finding? I want to know what led up to this conclusion," the president asked.

"It started with a number of kidnappings in the US and Canada," Director Wrangler began. "An agent in Denver found enough similarities to conclude it was an organized activity, including drug smuggling and trafficking. Last Wednesday, a car exploded in Eagle County, Colorado, killing three people. The FBI got involved, and on Thursday, a call came to the agent who had studied the kidnappings and who was in Eagle. The call came from a woman calling for help. She was in Avon, Colorado, only about twenty miles from the car explosion. Several agents responded and found the caller, a Russian woman, and two unconscious girls, both about four years old."

The director continued giving a detailed report of what had transpired up to the point where the girls had been reunited with their families. When finished, he sat back. He was glad he had it all written down, and he handed copies of the briefing to all present.

"And all this happened between Wednesday and Sunday. Who is in charge there?" asked the president.

"Locally in the field, Special Agent Linda Crawford is in charge. She is also the agent who studied the many kidnappings and found they were linked," the director responded.

"And why was she in Eagle?" the president asked. "When the car exploded, nobody knew it was linked to any kidnappings, as I understood from your presentation."

The director cursed himself for not seeing that gap. "I do not have the answer, Mr. President. Let me call Denver and find out."

"Why don't you get Agent Crawford on the line? This whole thing is both complicated and important. I think we better get it straight from the source, and we will probably have many more questions."

A minute later, Linda was on the line. The president spoke first.

"Agent Crawford, I understand that you have had a busy weekend in Eagle. I want to congratulate you and your colleagues on what you have accomplished."

"Thank you, Mr. President. I'll let them all know," Linda said.

"Unfortunately, as much as I wish differently, it's now that the heavy lifting begins, and you have too much to contribute to sit on the bench. I want you here as soon as possible. Go to your hotel and get ready for pickup in the next half hour or so. But before we end this chat, why were you in Eagle after that car exploded? At first, it had no obvious connection to any kidnapping. Was it just a coincidence?"

"Not just a coincidence, Mr. President. We had a kidnapping attempt in Denver on Saturday two weeks ago. What we believe is a grandfather got to the kidnapper, tackled him, and killed him. The driver of the getaway car was a female police officer. We checked her communication and found an email from an Eagle County sheriff's office regarding the delivery of an 'item.' When we asked what that meant, she would not answer, and we took her in. She committed suicide in our holding cell a few hours later through a small pill hidden in a cavity, Russian style. When the explosion happened ten days later in Eagle County, our agent in charge sent me here. He doesn't believe much in coincidences."

After a moment, the president asked, "Why did you say you believed it was a grandfather? He must have clarified that, or am I missing something?"

"We never found that man or the child. They disappeared and have still not been located or identified. Most of the kids recognized the child and knew his name. Some also recognized the man, so they must live in the neighborhood. It's a complete mystery, Mr. President."

"Thank you, Agent Crawford. This story goes from bad to worse the more I hear. We have eight people dead within two weeks, if I counted right. Now I really look forward to seeing you here in a few hours. Goodbye, Agent Crawford."

The president looked out over the assembly. They had all heard the conversation. It explained how the whole thing unraveled but didn't change the conclusion that Russia was using its foreign delegation to attack the people of the host country. That was an act of war. Legally, it had only occurred in Canada, at least from what they knew at this point. But the US would not stand on the sidelines. They had stolen its children as well.

"I spoke with the PM," the president said. "He's as upset as I am, if not more so. I have invited him to Camp David tomorrow at noon to prepare a call to Mr. Lenkov on Wednesday morning.

You shall be there as well. I'm not inclined to bring in the entire National Security Council. This is not a discussion about policy or what to do. We know what to do. You're here because your departments are directly involved in our next steps: first, to put this under the highest security, and then, to prepare to react to Mr. Lenkov's response.

"My hope is that Lenkov has been sidestepped by some crazy people and does not know about this. We'll tell him that using his diplomatic delegation to harm the people in the host country is a hostile activity on the most serious level. It is an act of war, and our response will reflect that. On the other hand, if our kids come home, all this will be put under twenty years' classification. Any thoughts? And speak up. That's why you are here."

The secretary of state was the first to speak. "Mr. President, we must start with the assumption that Mr. Lenkov has been sidestepped, because there's nothing but potential disaster in it for him. But he is a very vain man, and he is always trying to look like a winner. We can do that by throwing in a contribution to his effort if needed—a billion dollars or something. That will tickle his weak ego."

"A very good point, thank you. Anybody else?"

The secretary of homeland security was next. "Mr. President, this has the highest security for obvious reasons. Now, we have to alert the coast guard, the navy, and the air force to check every vessel that leaves the West Coast, from Alaska to California, starting ASAP. A lot of people have to be brought in, under secrecy, of course. Unfortunately, we know that there will be leaks, with so many individuals in the know."

"Thank you. Again, a good point. Here are my thoughts. As far as we know, those people have used Oregon, Washington State, and British Columbia for water smuggling. It will take them a while to set up new channels. We're talking weeks rather than days. My question is, can we limit this to the coast guard in Oregon and Washington, at least till we have Mr. Lenkov's response?"

"That would be a lot easier to arrange and will give us minimum disadvantage, if any. I will talk to the admiral after the meeting and request an iron curtain as of tomorrow at midnight. Thank you, sir."

It was quiet. The president spoke again.

"Thanks for your thoughts. As you heard earlier, Agent Crawford is on her way. We need to hear every piece of her story. I've decided to invite her to a private dinner when she arrives. I do not know what else can be picked up, but I would not risk missing anything. You are invited. That's all for now."

*   *   *

The first thing Linda did after the call was to find Steve and tell him he was in charge. She had been called to DC right away on a military jet from Eagle's airport. The president wanted every detail of this abduction scandal.

"Congratulations, Linda. And don't forget that a trip to DC to meet the president always comes with a one-way ticket. Good luck. We'll miss you."

They both laughed.

On her way to Eagle's airport, she called Mark. He was not available. He was probably researching, teaching, or doing who knows what. She left a message that she would call from DC when she arrived.

It was a fast and comfortable flight. An air force attendant offered some snacks and water. They landed at Joint Base Andrews, where a limo to the White House waited. There she was led to a guest room and asked to wait for someone to contact her. There were no time slots; it could be a few minutes or a few hours. She was recommended to make herself comfortable.

Linda freshened up and then called Mark again. Now he answered.

"Hi, darling. So, you are on the way to DC. Who are you going to see there?"

"I'm already in my room in the White House, Mark. I got here on a military jet and have been invited to dinner with the president. I am not comfortable at all. Say something to calm my nerves, darling."

"Can't do that, sweetheart. Nerves are good, within limits of course, and yours always are. Call me when it's over and let me know how it went. I'm not going to ask the nature of your conversation. I already know what it's about, and that's enough. Love you, darling."

"Love you too, Mark. You have already calmed me a lot. Bye, darling."

Linda sat down and looked around the room. It was not large, not one of the famous rooms that heads of state slept in, but it was comfortable, and it was in the White House. She felt appreciated and uncomfortable at the same time.

There was a soft knock on the door. A well-dressed young man bowed and invited her to follow him to the dining room. Of course, with a two-hour time difference, dinner was earlier here. How had she forgotten that simple fact? Those nerves again.

They arrived in the dining room. There were several men and one woman gathered and chatting. They introduced themselves and handed her their business cards. They were the secretary of state, secretary of defense, and the director of the FBI, Aaron Wrangler, who greeted her warmly. "I am very pleased to meet you, Agent Crawford. You are a greatly appreciated member of the FBI family," he said. The last to greet her was the secretary of homeland security, the lone lady in the group.

Linda was happy to end up next to a woman. They immediately started to talk about important things. Yes, the trip was very comfortable, like the limo and the room. She already liked DC, at least the White House part of it. A good, solid laugh from the secretary. Some ice broken—a good start.

The president entered, and all talking stopped. He immediately came up and greeted Linda. He gently moved her to a seat next to his while he inquired about her trip and accommodation. Linda felt relaxed, like she was among friends. She also knew it could all change in a heartbeat.

When all were seated, the president turned to Linda.

"Agent Crawford, you are very welcome to this important meeting. It's also secret. Nothing can leave this room, with the possible exception of the menu," he said lightheartedly. "What happened in Colorado is both scary and impressive, with Russia coming here and stealing our most valuable resource—our children—and how the FBI in Colorado has taken it all down in a matter of four or five days. Tomorrow, a Canadian delegation headed by the prime minister is coming to town to work out a joint response to President Lenkov, demanding the children back. It is imperative that we have all the facts about the Colorado operation, and you have been invited here to present those facts."

Soup was brought in, and the president told Linda that she could eat the soup and bread in peace. Afterward, they would all be anxious to hear her story.

Linda had ordered an iced tea and enjoyed a delicious lobster bisque with cheese crackers. She ate all she could find around her, well aware that this might be her entire White

House dinner. When she was done and wiped her lips, the president turned to her.

"Agent Crawford, the floor is yours, and we are all ears. You can sit, you can stand, you can walk—whatever makes you comfortable. But you cannot run out."

There was some laughter around the table as Linda stood up.

"Thank you, Mr. President, for inviting me here. I choose to stand, at least till I get my nerves under control. It all started about a month ago, when the agent in charge of our Denver office, Tom Baker, asked me to investigate a number of kidnappings in the northwestern US. It was not difficult to see that they were related: They were all white children between four and five years old from middle-class neighborhoods; they were all abducted in public areas in broad daylight with no witnesses and no random notes. They just disappeared, and nobody asked for any money."

Linda continued and gave a detailed account of what had transpired over the following four days until they found proof of Russia's involvement. It took well over a half hour. The room was totally quiet as she sat down. Nobody talked and nobody ate. After a long pause, the president spoke.

"Thank you, Agent Crawford. That was the most unusual briefing I've ever heard. I forgot the food, and I don't think I am the only one. There is only one thing that leaves a question in my mind. That person who gave your name and number to Tanya's Russian cousin seems to have a few things to tell us. That person is not our enemy, more likely our best friend, just like the two Russian cousins. Those cousins are probably here on some kind of visa. If they go back to Russia, they will not live very long. We have to take care of them. Citizenship, witness protection, whatever it takes. Agent Crawford, I ask you to do what you can to find the missing link here and also assure

Tanya that we will be proud to have her and her cousin as US citizens. Any other questions around the table?"

It was quiet for a few moments. Then the director of the FBI stood up.

"Agent Crawford, that was a very captivating presentation. I'm very impressed by your accomplishment, and I look forward to seeing you soon again. Thank you."

He applauded, and everyone, including the president, stood up and joined in. Linda didn't know what to say or do. She just sat and felt overwhelmed. Then the president turned to her.

"You probably realize that everything you said was recorded. As I mentioned earlier, we have a meeting tomorrow with our Canadian friends to hammer out a joint message to Mr. Lenkov. Your testimony tonight is the only solid proof we have of Russia's involvement and guilt. Without it, we couldn't even have this meeting. You have helped your country tremendously today. I may not see you in the next few days, but I look forward to the next opportunity. Thank you, Agent Crawford, and safe travels home." He shook her hand and left.

When the president was gone, the room relaxed. Everyone came up and congratulated her, and the director invited her over to the FBI office a block away for a drink and introduction to some colleagues. It was only a little past seven, and with nothing else to do, she happily accepted.

The following morning, Linda decided to fly home and see Mark for a day. She had been gone since Wednesday, and it was now Tuesday. She needed to change her clothes and sleep in her own bed, if only for one night. She felt mentally drained after yesterday's events. The same jet took her back to Denver. Mark took the afternoon off and met her at the airport. It seemed like months since she'd last seen him.

Chapter 15

Alina's phone buzzed just before ten with another message from Uncle Igor. She looked at Alex.

"They are leaving in an hour. If we are at the meeting point by seven tonight, they can meet us. What shall we do?" she asked.

She handed the phone with the coordinates to Alex, who put them into the plotter. The meeting point was exactly thirty-four miles straight west of their current location.

"I checked the fuel a couple of times during the night," Alex answered after some moments. "We only used less than half the tank, so we do not need to fill up. If we go to meet them and change our minds, we can always turn around. If we wait an hour, the option is lost. Let's go!"

Alex started the engine and pulled the anchor, and they were on their way. It was still a light northeasterly wind. The first leg out of the bay was about half an hour in a northeasterly direction. They should be at the meeting point very close to seven o'clock, barring any unforeseen events. Well back in the wide strait, he put the boat on an exactly westerly course and showed Alina how she should stay the course.

"That's easy. Just keep the W on the compass pointing forward," she said, smiling.

They decided on a late lunch around two.

"Could I take a little nap before then?" Alex asked.

"Of course you can," Alina said. "You're the captain."

He told her that the sun was too bright in the cockpit, so he went down to the cabin to nap. The forward bunk was the darkest and, more importantly, out of Alina's sight. That was also where his backpack with the shotgun was stored. Alex assembled and loaded the gun, put six shells in his windbreaker, and then walked back and put the gun in the foul-weather cabinet next to the companionway. He then returned to his forward bunk for his "nap," or rather, for time to think.

At two o'clock, he got up and opened the cabin hatch about two inches. They had passed Cape Flattery, the northwesternmost point of the continental US, and had the Cape Flattery Lighthouse due south. It also meant that the waves had changed as they got out into the Pacific Ocean.

The weather forecast called for a slight increase in the wind, overcast, and a drop in temperature by a couple of degrees. By and large, it was the same weather they had gotten used to.

The water was busy, with all kinds of boats and ships going to and coming from both Seattle and Vancouver. The Cape Flattery Lighthouse was the rounding point for the vast majority, with Alaska to the north and the rest of the world to the south and southwest. The occasional fishing boat would go straight out.

At six o'clock, Alex checked the binoculars, trying to spot a fishing boat heading in their direction. They were more than ten miles away from any boat traffic, and nothing was heading their way. By 6:30, he began to give up hope—or maybe *get* hope. For him, it would be just wonderful to head back to Neah Bay, fill the fuel and water tanks, and then rest for a day or two before starting their journey north to Alaska.

It was a quarter to seven when he spotted a sport fishing boat coming toward them at high speed. That couldn't be right, for traveling to Russia! The boat—or rather, the ship—began slowing down a few hundred feet away. It slowly turned so they would have the aft starboard for docking. It was a huge sport fishing boat, about a hundred feet long and almost as tall.

Alex looked for a man who met Alina's description of her uncle. He was not around to welcome his niece. Major red flag! He could only see three middle-aged men in black uniforms: two on the open sky bridge, controlling the boat, and one waiting to assist them with the docking—with a very serious face.

Alex had put a line at the bow and taught Alina how to throw it, in case that was the docking they chose. Now he told her to carefully go up and prepare the maneuver. The waves were not high, but their little boat was still rolling in the wake of the sport fishing boat.

Alex was standing in the cockpit, steering the boat toward the man, ready to catch Alina's line. Just before she threw it, his peripheral vision caught a glimpse of a man behind the glass doors on the main deck. He carried an AK-47.

When the man caught the line, Alex bent down under the sprayhood and put the gear in neutral. Instead of standing back up, he continued down into the cabin. He had the shotgun out in no time and pointed it through the hatch opening. Alina was out of the line of fire, forcefully dragged by the man toward the door on the lower deck. And just as bad, the man had not tied the docking line! The picture was suddenly crystal clear.

The man with the AK-47 was out the door, looking down at the sprayhood and ready to shoot when Alex stood up. The man didn't live long enough to get a chance to fire.

The two men up on the open sky bridge were looking down, now standing close enough to each other so their bodies touched. They couldn't see their dead comrade from their position and probably thought he was the shooter. Alex aimed right between them. They both fell, maybe not dead, but they were out.

Another man appeared behind the first man on the main deck, also armed with an AK-47. Alex was now back in the companionway and reloaded. The man emptied the magazine into the cabin hatch and top. His second magazine was emptied in the same area. When that was empty and he stopped to push in the third magazine, Alex peeked up over the sprayhood and shot him. The man didn't even have time to know that his life had ended.

The man who had manhandled Alina came back out the door on the lower level. He was also carrying an AK-47. Goodness, how many were there? He also emptied the magazine into the cabin. *Why not? Nobody takes shelter under a sprayhood!* When he reloaded, his life ended.

Alex crawled down into the companionway for his second reload. He stayed down, waiting for the next shot. Maybe somebody got smart and stood waiting for him, and he was not ready to die just yet. After maybe five minutes, he carefully looked through a rip in the sprayhood. He saw the transom of the big boat; it was at least two hundred feet away. The big boat was slowly idling away.

He sat down in the companionway to rest, to wait for a greater distance to build, and to think. First, it may not be over. It was still possible that a couple of survivors were planning revenge. The cabin was a mess, but he couldn't see any holes below the waterline. The little boat was still dry. He peeked out. The distance had increased, and nobody was around. He decided to spend a few more minutes in hiding to check himself. There was blood all around, and there weren't many suspects.

Then he remembered Alina; his single-minded quest for survival had excluded even her from his mind. He needed to find help, and the coast guard was his only option. The nav station was shot to pieces, but the handheld marine radio he had bought as backup might work. It was still in its box up front. He found it, put in batteries, and activated it. Its range was only a few miles, primarily designed for marina use, but the coast guard station at Leah Bay might still pick up the signal; they had sophisticated equipment.

He went up in the cockpit. About five minutes had passed, and the sport fishing boat was a quarter of a mile away. He turned to channel sixteen and started calling, "Mayday, Mayday!" He paused to listen for a response. "Mayday, Mayday!" Suddenly, there was some crackling in the radio, and a voice came through.

"This is the coast guard. What is your position?"

Alex gave his coordinates and continued, "Officer, I am fine. No problems. I met a large sport fishing boat with a woman waving for help. I'm on a sailboat and cannot assist. The boat is slowly moving northeast about a quarter mile from me now. It flies a Russian flag and has Russian letters on the transom. There are no other people in sight. Over."

"Thank you, Captain, we will check it out. Over and out."

Alex was surprised. They didn't ask for his name or anything specific. On the other hand, he had never made a Mayday call before. The engine had been idling all along, and with no plans where to go, he turned east, back toward land. He had a few hours to think and to patch himself up.

There was still some daylight left. Alex started to check the damage to his body. The adrenaline had numbed all his pain senses, but that would soon change. He found a gash on the top of his head. His cap, windbreaker, sweater, and shirt were soaked in blood. His left arm and his right leg had cuts. Not too bad, considering the bloodbath he had been through. He went down and found the first aid bag, a bed sheet, a couple of gallon jugs of water, a few towels, a pot, and a roll of masking tape, and brought it all up to the cockpit. The boat had again changed direction, and he rigged some lines to stabilize the course.

Alex started to fix his body one wound at a time. He started with the simplest and lowest on the right leg. A splinter was sticking out. He pulled it, washed the wound with water, poured some alcohol over it, and put on some Neosporin and a band-aid. Then he moved on to his left arm. He took off his life jacket, windbreaker, sweater, and shirt. The wound was close to his shoulder but had no foreign objects inside. His windbreaker was also ripped. It could have been by anything, even a bullet. He washed the wound, poured some alcohol on it, and then applied Neosporin. It required a couple of gauze patches and two feet of masking tape to stay put.

About twenty minutes after his call, two coast guard helicopters approached the sport fishing boat. It was now about a mile away, and the light was fading. Alex had to use his binoculars and pull the speed down to idle to be able to see what had happened. Several officers, maybe six or seven of them, were lowered on board. The helicopters remained. Alex was partly relieved. Help had arrived, but he still didn't know Alina's condition.

Alex increased the speed again to four knots. He started to pat his head and work on a plan. The first thing to do was a no-brainer. The gun and ammunition had to be packed and ready to go overboard at first sight of a coast guard vessel. That was soon done, and the boat stayed the course.

He had fuel to get back to Neah Bay, but the boat's condition was a giveaway. Tomorrow, everybody will be looking for the shooter of five people on the sport fishing boat. Three or four empty magazines showed that the shooter's boat was messed up too. The great little boat had to go down before daylight.

He had to check the dinghy. He again slowed to idle, put his life jacket and a safety line on, and crawled up on deck. The dinghy was inflated and tied down forward of the mast. It was not hit. No shots had passed in front of the mast, at least not at the point where the dinghy rested.

The docking line had been floating in the water since he left the big boat. It was only fifteen feet long, so it did not pose a risk of getting into the propeller. Still, it was in the wrong place, so he fished it up and secured it. He untied the dinghy and tied its docking line to a cleat by the cockpit. When it was time to abandon the boat, he just had to push it into the water.

The outboard on the transom railing was also out of line of fire. Even the gas tank tied to the railing was undamaged. There had been no stray bullets. They had all gone where they had been aimed—into the cabin side and top. Thank God for good shooters!

A plan started to form. Alex would head southeast and approach land somewhere twenty to thirty miles down the coast from Neah Bay. He would pack everything he needed in his backpack, sink the boat about a mile out, take the dinghy to shore, hide it, and become one of the hundreds of hikers in Olympic National Park. The season was still more than a month away, but there were always some early risers, people who embraced solitude, enjoyed being part of nature, and watch it wake up from its winter sleep.

From there, he would hike to some town and get his head wound taken care of. He still did not know what happened. He had not felt anything hit him, and yet it seemed like both his head and his arm had been grazed by bullets. He would explain that he had stumbled and hit a rock.

All the boat's electrical systems were dead. He had no plotter and no lights, not even navigation lights. The only things working were the magnetic compass, the handheld spotlight, and the handheld VHF—his lifesavers.

He had to navigate through boat traffic unseen by other boats. Maybe he would not even be spotted on their radar, considering the small size of *Springtime*. He was still outside the heavy traffic channel, but at some point, he had to cross it. Worst case, he still could wave his spotlight.

He patted his head. It was already dark, but that made no difference; he couldn't see the top of his head anyway. The warm, knitted cap was soaked in blood and partially glued to the head and his hair. He rolled the bed sheet around his neck to keep his clothes as dry as possible and soaked a towel in fresh water. It took about half an hour to soak the cap enough to pull it off. Still, chunks of hair followed. Then he put a clean, wet towel over the wound for about another half hour to loosen the dirt enough to clean most of it out. He poured half of the alcohol bottle into the wound and let it sting. It was not pleasant at all, but he knew he was alive. Then he applied most of the Neosporin and several sterile gauze patches. Finally, he secured it all with several feet of blue masking tape wrapped around his head in different directions. He was glad the mirror was shot to pieces.

It was past midnight, and he was approaching the traffic channel. He was some distance from any ship and still more than ten miles from shore. Ideally, he wanted to sink the boat a mile out between two and three o'clock. It would be deep enough—a few hundred feet—and he would get to shore well before first light.

To sink the boat, he needed to open all three seacocks and shoot a few holes through the hull to speed up the process. He had thirteen shells left and shot them all three to six inches above the waterline. He was far enough from land not to worry about the shots being heard. And all the shootings were done in the cabin.

He was surprised by the low number of ships heading south. It was like they all anchored up for the night. When he was in the traffic channel, the only ships he had to worry about were northbound, and they were all many miles away. The journey back to shore was a lot easier than he had expected.

Right around 2:30 a.m., he killed the engine. The distance to shore was approximately a mile, and he was well inside any boat traffic. He closed the seacocks and cut the water hoses to the head, galley, and engine. Then he reopened the valves. Water quickly started to flow into the cabin.

Alex pushed the dinghy into the water and tied it close to the cockpit on the lee side. He put in the outboard, gas tank, oars, and backpack, and then, with some difficulty, himself.

He hooked the outboard to the mounting board, connected the gas hose, and pumped the bulb, and then—the moment of truth. He had already run the motor when he checked it all out two long days ago, or maybe three. It was all a blur with everything between love and war over a few days.

The outboard started after the third pull. With a sting of sadness, he untied the line from *Springtime* and aimed for land. The ride was a little choppy, and he ran at half speed. After about fifteen minutes, the water calmed down, but he maintained the speed and low noise level; no need to risk waking any campers on the beach.

The prop hit the sandy bottom maybe thirty feet out. He killed the outboard and pushed with an oar until he had to get in the water and pull the dinghy up on the beach. By the time he had pulled it into the dense vegetation and got his backpack out, the time was 4:30.

His estimate was that he landed twenty-five miles south of Flattery Rocks. There was nothing but nature around. He got his backpack and started to walk down the beach. When he saw the first faint light of day, he looked for a flat spot among the trees and bushes. He found a spot, got the tent up, and fell asleep on top of his sleeping bag, fully dressed and totally exhausted.

Chapter 16

The first guardsmen lowered onto the sport fishing boat were shocked. It was a ninety-two-foot yacht, beautiful from every angle, with all the bells and whistles anybody could dream up. And then, dead bodies everywhere, with blood dripping from the open flybridge all the way down to the fishing cockpit three decks below. The yacht was still moving forward at idle speed, with not a living soul in sight.

One guardsman took control of the yacht at the enclosed bridge as the others entered the salon on the main deck. There were comfortable couches, easy chairs, a long bar, a dining area, and a kitchen—and nobody around. They headed down to the staterooms. They counted one empty room, then two, then three. The fourth door was locked from the outside. They unlocked the door and got even more surprises. Inside the room was a middle-aged lady and three young children sitting on a bed. Lying on another bed was an old man, seemingly asleep.

All stared at the guardsmen, first in horror like it was their turn to die; then, gradually, their faces showed relief. A couple of guardsmen pulled out a few energy bars and gave them to the woman, who shared them with the small children. There were sudden smiles and hope on their faces.

Another guardsman, a doctor, came down and set up a makeshift examination area in one of the staterooms. He went back to the room with the people and turned toward the woman.

"I'm Dr. Fleming. I'm going to check on the children to see that they are OK. Could you help me with them? And what's your name?"

"Alina. Yes, I can help," she said. She took the children to the examination room. She picked up one child after another and put them on her lap. The doctor checked their hearts, eyes, mouths, and limbs.

When he was done, he said, "They seem lethargic, almost asleep. Are they on any kind of medication?"

"Probably," Alina said, "but I am not sure. I only got here half an hour ago."

The doctor heard her accent and realized she had misunderstood him. He didn't need to check Alina; she had shown her presence when she assisted him. She just needed to work on her English.

Last to be checked was the old man. The doctor walked back into the first cabin. Alina went with him. He looked down at the old man and checked his pulse. He turned toward Alina, trying to decide what to say so he was not misunderstood again. Alina spoke first.

"He is dead. He died a few minutes ago. It was his choice. He is my uncle."

She had an accent, but her English was flawless. The doctor realized she had not misunderstood him at all fifteen minutes ago. He had quickly checked the dead men when they came on board and estimated the time of their demise to be well under an hour before their arrival. Alina must have gotten on the boat at about the time the shootings happened. He was utterly puzzled but decided it was not his concern, not at that moment.

The captain who led the guardsmen declared the vessel seaworthy. There were no leaks, and all instruments and lights worked. The engines had been humming all along, and they had fuel to cross an ocean. The huge sport fishing boat could travel back to the Coast Guard Air Station Port Angeles under its own power.

As they traveled back, the guardsmen brought all the bodies down to the fishing cockpit and then hosed down the entire superstructure. This was done for safety but also revealed a spectacularly beautiful ship.

They returned to the coast guard station after about three hours of travel and killed the engines right at midnight. As the guardsmen were getting ready to disembark the ship, Dr. Fleming spoke to the captain in charge. "These children have been drugged, probably with some sleep aid. They are now deep asleep, and it makes no sense to wake them up to be moved to another sleeping quarter. I suggest the children and the lady remain on board. Besides, we cannot find a more comfortable place for them to sleep in." The captain agreed, and Dr. Fleming went down to Alina, who was in the stateroom with the children.

"We are ready to disembark now, but you and the children can stay here. You're well-guarded and totally safe. But out of curiosity, why are the children here, and why were they drugged?"

"They have been kidnapped in the US and Canada and were being shipped to Russia. They were drugged to forget their parents," she responded.

The doctor was speechless. A search for young, stolen children on all vessels leaving the US and Canada had started only a few minutes before. And here the children were, at least a few of them, thanks to some people who had attacked this vessel five hours before the midnight start time. And Alina was one of those people. Who was this woman, and what happened to the rest of the group? There were several empty magazines on this vessel, indicating a virtual bloodbath by the time Alina came on board. He needed to share this with the commander right away.

"Thank you for that information. I hope you will sleep well here, and I look forward to talking more in the morning."

The doctor left and found the commander in his office. The blockade that had just taken effect meant that the entire coast guard station was up and running. He relayed that the vessel they had brought back had three kidnapped children on board. Considering the intensity of the whole operation, it might be reason to share this finding with the admiral. The commander agreed and made the call.

Chapter 17

The president's and prime minister's meeting at Camp David was somber and focused on one thing only—the message to President Lenkov. They agreed to make the call at nine o'clock the next morning. That would be four in the afternoon in Moscow and hopefully before vodka started to flow before dinner.

The message to be delivered was along the lines the president had outlined the previous day. If the US and Canada get the children back, all would be classified. If they didn't get their children back, Russia would be at war with the US and Canada.

The two delegations sat down for dinner at seven o'clock. There were twelve people around the table. The president said a few words, and they all started to enjoy the delicious food and matching wines. Dinner talk flowed without effort. They were all among friends. After dinner, they continued to talk and play pool. Wine and after-dinner drinks had helped to ease their worries. Lenkov really didn't have any options; he had to return the children.

At 10:50, a well-decorated navy commander entered the room and walked up to the president. She had an important message. The president looked a bit annoyed but mostly concerned. They left the room. A couple of minutes later, they both came back. The president announced that the commander had a message that concerned them all.

She said, "Around seven o'clock Pacific time, a vessel belonging to the Russian consulate in Vancouver was attacked on international waters thirty miles west of Cape Flattery, Washington, and thirty miles south of Vancouver Island. Five people were shot dead. One person died from other causes. Four people were unharmed: a middle-aged woman, two young boys, and one young girl. Their ages are not yet determined."

After a long silence, Director Wrangler asked, "Who attacked them? It couldn't have been the coast guard or the navy."

The commander answered, "We do not have that information, sir. A man called the coast guard at four minutes past seven Pacific time and stated that a woman on the vessel had been waving for help. The coast guard responded to the distressed vessel. However, nobody could have waved for help. They were all dead or locked up in a stateroom."

"Any word on how they were attacked?" the president asked.

"We do not have all the details, sir, but the preliminary information is that they all were shot by a shotgun."

The president just slumped down in a chair with his drink, staring straight out. After a long while, he muttered, seemingly to himself and barely loud enough for the others to hear, "It's the same guy in all these places. He shoots up the bad guys and then calls law enforcement to come in and clean up. But who is he and why does he do it? He is putting his life on the line . . . it is personal to him. He is our best friend, and I want to find him!"

The president stood up slowly and with an exhausted look on his face. He turned to the prime minister.

"I need some rest. Let's have breakfast at seven and try to figure out if this changes our call to Lenkov. I hope you sleep well tonight, my friend."

As he started to leave, he stopped and looked at the FBI director.

"Aaron, make sure that the people who attacked this vessel are covered by the witness protection we put in place for the Russian ladies, at least till we know who they are. And get the names and the descriptions of all the abducted children before our call."

Chapter 18

Linda enjoyed the evening with Mark; she could finally relax. She even thought about calling Steve and telling him she would stay home another day. But that didn't happen. At 9:30, her phone rang. It was the director—never a good sign.

"Good evening, sir," Linda answered.

"Good evening, Linda. We just got word that a vessel belonging to the Russian consulate in Vancouver has been attacked on international waters west of Seattle. The entire crew was shot dead by a shotgun. The shooter has not been found. One Russian woman and three young, English-speaking children were found on board, unharmed and locked up. The woman's name is Alina. I suggest you go to Seattle first thing tomorrow morning. Take our plane. I look forward to your report, and so does the president. Good night, Linda."

Linda put her phone down. She had hardly said a word, not even good night. Mark looked at her. He had never seen her so perplexed. He stayed quiet.

After a while, she looked up at him and said slowly, "I need a glass of water, please."

Mark got water for both, then sat back and waited. Linda drank some and then put the glass down. She had regained her normal posture.

"That was an interesting call. The shooter from Vail and Eagle has done it again, and this time out in the Pacific Ocean, on international waters. Shot the whole crew dead with a shotgun. And just like before, there's not a trace of the shooter, except this time, he left three unharmed children and his sidekick, Alina, on board.

"But a *shotgun*, Mark. You kill birds from a few hundred feet away. To kill a person, you have to be within two hundred feet. He had to be right there, on the boat. Did he come in a speed boat, and nobody reacted? That's possible if they knew and trusted him. But why leave Alina behind? It doesn't make any sense. Guess where I'm going tomorrow, darling?"

Linda got up and hugged Mark, now with a smile on her face.

Chapter 19

The call to President Lenkov the following morning began with the US president explaining the reason for the call.

"President Lenkov, for about six months, Russia has systematically abducted American and Canadian children," he opened. "At least seven American and four Canadian children, all four or five years old, have been kidnapped and transported out through the Russian consulate in Vancouver, Canada, most likely by sea vessels. Through our efficient law enforcement, five of these children have been recovered over the last week, but the remaining six have been smuggled out of the two countries.

"The Canadian prime minister and I believe and hope that this has been done without your involvement and knowledge. Both countries expect the children's immediate return, and if that is done, it will be proof of your non-involvement. It will be classified, and Russia will avoid the world's reaction to the scandal.

"If the children are not returned, it will show that this crime has been endorsed by the Russian president and that Russia has used its diplomatic establishment to cause harm to the people of the host country. That is an act of war declared by Russia against the US and Canada. Mr. President, the prime minister and I want to hear your response."

A long period of total silence followed. Then a raspy voice was heard, not from a translator, but from Mr. Lenkov himself.

"It is the most stupid thing I ever heard," he said in slow and broken English. "We don't need your children. We know how to make them here in Russia better than you do. You will get your children back, and I want classification for thirty years. If we have an understanding, I will ask my minister of foreign affairs to arrange it. Is that all?"

"We agree on the classification, but our information points at your minister of foreign affairs as the man behind all this." There was another long pause.

"I will ask his successor to arrange it. Is that all?"

"We look forward to working with your new minister of foreign affairs. Thank you, Mr. President."

There was a deep sigh of relief when the call was over. The president, the prime minister, their secretaries, the FBI director, their translators, and their assistants high-fived, hugged, and congratulated each other. What a day!

The next day, the Russian state news channel reported the unfortunate passing of the country's respected and beloved minister of foreign affairs. He had sadly tripped over the railing of his twelfth-floor balcony.

Chapter 20

The following morning, Linda got up at six for a quick stretch and breakfast before she headed to the airport again for a private flight, this time to Seattle. This was the third flight in a row with her as the only passenger. She decided she could easily get used to her own plane.

She landed on the airstrip at the Coast Guard Air Station Port Angeles at 9:00 a.m. The guardsman who met her explained that the entire operation was under top security, and everybody was kept at the station. That included three young children, who were sleeping in a stateroom on board the captured vessel under the watch of a coast guard doctor and a lady.

Linda was full of expectations for her first meeting with Alina. Who was this Russian woman who had traveled all over the US and, together with an unidentified person, shot up and destroyed an entire international crime organization? In her mind, she saw a hardened, muscular woman.

Linda entered the yacht and was guided to the salon. She was amazed by the opulence and comfort of the fishing boat. She stood there and just looked around at the bar, furniture, TV, aquarium, and decorations.

An attractive, slender, middle-aged woman came up the stairs. *She must be a nurse or a guardswoman coming to take me to Alina*, Linda thought. The woman walked right up to her and held out her hand.

"Hi, Linda, I am so glad to finally meet you. My name is Alina. I think you met my cousin, Tanya," the woman said.

Linda shook her hand. Alina spoke perfect English with only a slight accent. She was a confident, open person, and Linda immediately felt comfortable in her company.

"Alina, the pleasure is mine. I have been looking forward to meeting you for a very long time, a whole week now," Linda said.

Alina smiled and then turned very serious as she spoke. "Linda, I have something very important to talk to you about. Can we do that right now?"

"Of course, we can. What is it?"

"Let's go downstairs."

Linda followed Alina down the stairs and into a stateroom. A heavy man was lying on the bed. He looked dead.

"This is my uncle," Alina said. "He was the Consul General at the Russian Consulate in Vancouver. About six months ago he was ordered by the minister of foreign affairs, his boss's boss, to help transport children from here to Russia. Stolen children. He thought that was a horrible thing and did everything he could to stay away from it, but that does not work in our system. He knew it would end badly, both for him and for Russia. He did as little as possible and lost his job. Six children have been sent to Russia, and there are three children here who are safe now. He kept a record of all the children, and I want you to have it, so it does not get lost." Alina got an envelope out of a briefcase and gave it to Linda.

"This will show you when they were shipped and to which city in Russia. It also shows the names of the boats and the people who took them when they got there," she explained. "My uncle gave this to me last night as soon as I got here. Then he said he must say goodbye. Back in Russia he would be killed, and if he stayed here his wife and children in Russia would be killed. Only when they see his dead body will they stop hunting his family. I don't know exactly when he took the pill. He didn't want me to get upset, but suddenly he fell asleep. He did it to save his family."

When she finished, her grief and emotions took over. Tears welled up in her eyes and she sat down by her uncle. After a while Linda sat down and put her arms around her. That's how they were sitting for a long time, nobody cared how long, until Alina slowly rose and gave Linda a hug. "Thank you," she said simply as they both started to make themselves ready to meet the world again.

When they got up in the salon, they met Dr. Fleming in the company of the Coast Guard Station's commanding officer. The Commander immediately walked over to Linda. The creds around her neck gave her away.

"Agent Crawford, I'm Commander Hartman. You're very welcome to our station. We are all very impressed by your work." He then turned to Alina, whom he recognized from Dr. Flemings description. "Alina, I heard about your loss. My deepest condolences to you and your family. You should also know that we are all immensely thankful for what you've done to put an end to this horrible crime. The entire station will do what we can to make your stay her as comfortable as we possible."

After a moment, Dr. Fleming said, "The children are ready to move off the boat and to Seattle Children's Hospital for a final checkup."

Alina added, "My uncle can be moved as well. I have said my goodbye. But he must be moved to a Russian embassy. If they don't see his body, they will believe he is alive and hiding, and they will kill his family."

Both Dr. Fleming and Commander Hartman looked surprised.

Linda clarified, "Alina's uncle, the Consul General at the consulate in Vancouver, had been fired for insubordination and was arrested when the boat crossed into international waters. He had tried to sabotage their efforts to ship stolen children to Russia. He awaited prosecution there. If they believe he is alive here, his family will be prosecuted. We must make sure his body is delivered to a Russin embassy in D.C. or Ottawa, and FBI can take care of that.

"Alina gave me a document a few minutes ago. She received it from her uncle before he passed. It gives us the whereabouts of all six children that have been shipped to Russia. There are no children unaccounted for, so this shipping blockade may not be needed anymore."

Commander Hartman was elated over the news and had to leave immediately to take the necessary steps to cancel the blockade. He thanked the ladies and was gone. Dr. Fleming looked a bit lost, but Linda saved the moment: "The three children will soon be ready to be returned to their parents. We went through that in Colorado and developed a small routine to make the process simple for the parents. I could take care of that here as well. It's the only reward among all these tragedies."

"Thank you. We'll certainly accept that help," Dr. Fleming said. "I have to return to my hospital in Forks, the sooner the better."

When they were alone again, Linda told Alina they needed to talk somewhere quiet. Alina suggested the bridge one level up. It was perfect, very comfortable and private. When they were seated with a beautiful view across the water toward Vancouver Island, Linda spoke.

"First of all, I want you to know that this entire kidnapping tragedy has been classified. This is so we could get Mr. Lenkov's cooperation to get the children back. There has been no news, no press, nothing going out to the public. It will be sealed for thirty years. It also means there will be no legal processes against the people who have been involved in taking down those criminals. We know that you and at least one other person have done most, maybe all, of that work. You have so far saved five children and maybe all the kidnapped children when this is over.

"Our president is heavily involved. Two days ago, he asked me directly to find you and your partner. He will give you every protection, including US citizenship and new identities. My question is, Alina, what happened to your partner or partners last night? Both the president and I want to know that they are alive and can get help if needed."

Tears were again rolling down Alina's cheeks, and Linda felt terrible to cause this so soon after her tearful goodbye to her uncle. After a while, Alina said, "I believe he was killed last night. How could he not be? They kept shooting and shooting at our little boat as soon as I stepped onto this horrible thing. We both came to visit my uncle; he had invited us. I just wanted to see him again before he went home and retired. My friend and I talked about a life together here in the US. We were just visiting my uncle, and then we were going to sail to Alaska. We were so happy. How could this happen?"

Linda felt worse than at any other time, but her brain was still working. When Alina's sobbing started to ease, she asked, "If you just came to visit your uncle, how come the entire crew was shot dead?"

"I DO NOT KNOW!" Alina answered in a raised voice. "I have asked myself that already a hundred times. I cannot understand.

The gun was disassembled and packed. He must have known something because as soon as I stepped onto this boat, I saw a man step out from the salon with a gun to shoot him. Instead, *he* was shot before he could fire. Then all the others started to shoot. There were hundreds of shots. I was already downstairs in a bedroom and couldn't see, but I could hear. He must have shot them all, but he must also have been shot."

Linda waited a few seconds and then asked, "Who called the coast guard? The whole crew was dead, and you were all locked up."

Again, Alina answered, "I do not know. I cannot figure it out."

Linda said, "According to the coast guard, a man called right around seven o'clock. He said that a woman on this boat was waving for help. He couldn't help them because he was on a sailboat, and this boat was moving away too fast. That's why the coast guard came to you. But nobody on this boat could have waved; the crew was dead, you were locked up, and there was nobody else around. Alina, it was your friend that called. And if he had been seriously wounded, he would have asked the coast guard to help him also. I believe your friend is alive, and you and I will find him."

Alina looked at Linda with a mix of hope and disbelief. "My God, I hope you are right."

"What is your friend's name?" Linda asked.

"I'm sorry, but I cannot tell you. I promised that if we got separated, I would never tell his name until I knew he was dead. He was afraid his family would believe he was crazy if they found out what he had done. They would disown him, I think he said."

"I think I understand his reasoning. So, we have to find him without his name. Why not talk about your little boat?"

Alina smiled when Linda mentioned the boat. "I'd love to do that, but Linda, I slept four hours the night before and nothing last night. Can I please have a break?"

Linda jumped up. "My goodness, I'm so sorry. I have to find rooms for us both."

That was soon arranged, and both were taken to the guest quarters at the station. It was midafternoon, and lunch had been forgotten as well. Alina probably hadn't had any breakfast either. Linda arranged for a plate with sandwiches and fruit. Alina was already asleep when she came back, so Linda put the food on the little coffee table in her room.

She brought her own plate back to her room and sat down at the worktable to eat and to think. Her phone rang. It was the White House. She answered with mixed feelings of hope and another disaster.

"Good afternoon, Agent Crawford," the president started. "I want to share some very good news with you. We had a conversation with Mr. Lenkov this morning with the best possible result: All the children will come home. Lenkov had no idea about this scandal; it was all the work of his minister of foreign affairs. We are all extremely appreciative of your work, and I wanted to be the first to congratulate you and thank you."

"Thank you, Mr. President. I will pass this on to all involved."

"Good, and thanks again. Have a very good day. Goodbye, Agent Crawford."

Linda sat back and slowly started to eat her sandwich. If this had happened a day earlier, would Alina's uncle still be alive? After some wrestling with her emotions, she decided that the question was hypothetical. She must not let it ruin the very good news she had just received, but it could still be an issue when she shared it with Alina.

She finished her lunch and opened the envelope Alina gave her. She was curious to see what Alina's uncle had handed over before he ended his life. They were three full pages with a mix of English and Russian words. Still, the content was clear, and Linda felt a sting of sadness as she scanned the pages, sadness over a very decent man who gave his life to save these children, unknown to him.

The pages listed a total of eleven children in chronological order. There were no names, only numbers: the dates they had been abducted, their ages, and genders. They were in Russian, but from the children Linda had already seen, she could understand their meaning.

Then there were several dates and names. Again, Linda could understand some important parts: the names of boats and cities and the dates of shipments. That told her that the three children they now had on board were two American boys, one five years old and one four years old, and one four-year-old Canadian girl.

Looking at her own data and seeing the dates of abductions and shipments, she could determine which children had already been shipped to Russia. She now knew who the parents of the three children were and where they lived. Linda was excited. She went over to the ship where the children were getting ready to be transported to the hospital. They were now off any medication and were behaving as could be expected. They were crying, and it was difficult to dress them and get them ready.

Linda asked one of the female guardsmen if she could have a word with her. She showed her the papers with the dates of abductions, and on her own computer, the full names of the children, as well as their parents' and siblings' names.

They both went back to the stateroom where the children were getting ready. Linda told them they would soon see their families and siblings again, using both their names and the names of their family members. But first, they had to go and see a doctor. The sooner they were ready, the sooner all this would happen. When that was taken care of, the children could not move any faster.

When they were dressed and ready, Linda told the same officer that she would be glad to follow them to the hospital and contact the parents. This would be a repeat of the situation they had experienced less than a week ago in Colorado. The officer was relieved. She had no idea how this both happy and difficult process would be handled.

The only thing different this time was the Canadian girl. Linda called the commanding officer of the RCMP in Vancouver. It was a pleasant conversation.

"Good morning, Agent Crawford," the Commander said. "I just got a call from the Commissioner with the incredibly good news, and I want to personally thank you for your accomplishment."

"Thank you, Commander, and I have a question for you. One of the children we found last night is Canadian, from Edmonton. This evening, I will contact the parents in the US and inform them that their child has been found in good health and can be picked up at the children's hospital here. I would be happy to call the parents in Canada as well, if that is OK with you."

"Of course, that would be very helpful. You have the experience, and you have the child. Thank you, Agent Crawford, and good luck."

A couple of minutes later, Commander Hartman called Linda and said, "Agent Crawford, I just received the news about the president's call to Lenkov. I want to congratulate you and thank you. I also heard that you are taking the children to the hospital in Seattle. That's a very uncomfortable drive. Whether you go around the bay or by ferry, it takes hours. We can fly you there; just let us know when you're ready."

"Thank you, Commander," Linda answered. "I was a bit concerned about spending that time in a car with three abused children. I'm planning to contact the parents tonight, stay overnight in a hotel nearby, and hand over the children tomorrow, or whenever they can get there."

"I believe that is the most rewarding part of this entire ordeal. I wish you a very good time with both the children and parents. And when you are coming back here, just let us know and we will pick you up."

"Thank you very much, Commander. Can I ask how many people the chopper takes? I'm asking because the Russian woman, Alina, might be better off coming with us, if possible."

"I'll make sure that will be possible. The three children really only count as one. Best of luck with it all, Agent Crawford."

Linda walked over to Alina's room and woke her up. That took a while; she had a lot of sleep deprivation to compensate for. When she finally was somewhat awake, Linda said, "Alina, I'm taking the children to a hospital in Seattle. A helicopter is taking us, and we'll have a hotel room, so you can catch up on sleep. Would you like to come along?"

Alina was immediately up from her bed. She only needed a few minutes to pack her bag.

They walked back to the yacht and the children. Linda informed the two officers about the trip by helicopter. She then called the hospital and asked them to prepare for three children coming from the coast guard station. It took a minute, and then the operator came back.

"Is this in addition to the request by Dr. Fleming a couple of hours ago?"

"Oh, sorry, I was not aware of that. Thank you so much. We'll arrive within the hour at the helipad if somebody can meet us there. Everybody should be able to walk without assistance."

"You are all welcome. Goodbye."

The flight was a treat for the children. They pointed, talked, and laughed as they flew over islands, big ships, and parts of Seattle. They seemed to have totally forgotten the immediate past. Linda reflected on this as a therapeutic experience. Even upon arrival at the hospital, the children were polite and well-behaved—a huge difference in less than an hour.

Linda and Alina walked the short distance to the hotel. All was taken care of; they just had to see Linda's ID. They got their keys and walked up to their room. It was a big, beautiful suite with two bedrooms, one with two queen beds and one with a king. What a treat! *Thank you, coast guard!* Linda thought.

At six o'clock, Linda started to call the parents. That was a time when most people were home, and she got in touch with all three. Their reactions were similar: first, utterly sad voices, and moments later, when they grasped the significance of Linda's message, relief and joy.

The parents of the five-year-old boy lived in a southern suburb of Seattle. They drove over right away and arrived at the hospital a half hour later, only minutes after Linda and Alina got there. The doctor had left but had checked all the children and found them well. They were disturbed by their ordeal, yes, but not more than being back home would be the best remedy.

The administrative papers from the hospital had been signed. All that was left was the release document for the FBI. After the normal questions and answers, thanks, and tears of joy and gratitude, the family returned home.

Alina, like everybody else, enjoyed watching the little boy being reunited with his parents and siblings. She felt a bit satisfied that she had played a small part in making it happen. But her thoughts were with Alex. He was the one who had risked his life to take down this kidnapping organization, and now she didn't even know if he was alive, regardless of what Linda had tried to convince her.

The two remaining families showed up early Thursday afternoon. One family came from Missoula, Montana, and the other from Edmonton, Alberta. The Canadian family did not have a passport for their four-year-old daughter, but that was taken care of by the coast guard. They flew the family to the coast guard station in Vancouver. There, they stayed overnight and flew back to Edmonton the next morning.

Linda and Alina left the hospital at 5:30 p.m. and went to a nearby restaurant. For the first time in almost three weeks, Linda could relax. But Alina was in a different situation. Her partner had still not been found. Linda had decided never to bring up the fact that the Russian minister behind this tragedy was now burning in hell and that Alina's uncle's sacrifice might not have been necessary.

They flew back to the coast guard station late Friday morning. Linda's mission was over, but it didn't feel like it. The president had specifically asked her to bring back Alina's partner, or partners, who together with Alina had taken out at least eleven people and stopped this horrible crime activity. The only thing she knew was that it was one person, a man. Alina had clarified that. But nobody knew where to find him.

Chapter 21

Alex woke up at noon. The canopy kept the tent dark enough to let him sleep. What woke him were engines rumbling outside. He lifted the tent flap and peeked out. He was protected by trees and shrubs but could still see the water. There were three coast guard cutters about two hundred feet apart slowly moving south. On each were two or three guardsmen checking the water and the beach. They had already traveled past his spot without detecting him.

He laid back and picked up his sea chart. The only things it showed were the immediate coastline, creeks, seaside towns, and navigation markers. But that was enough. There was a small town, La Push, which he estimated to be five to eight miles south. In La Push, he would have radio and telephone reception and get the news. Hopefully they had a medical clinic as well. The head wound was bothering him. It had never stopped bleeding. The pain was getting worse, and he recognized the symptoms of a growing inflammation.

He ate some handfuls of trail mix, drank water, and called it lunch. Then he packed up his tent and other belongings and started to walk down the beach. He felt tired. The walk was slow. He decided to call it a day at four o'clock. He found a flat spot among the trees, set up his tent, and cooked one of his freeze-dried beef stews. He fell asleep at six o'clock.

After more than twelve hours of undisturbed sleep, Alex woke up rested but with a splitting headache. He got up, got some trail mix and water, and resumed his hike. Despite his long sleep, his pace was slow. He did not feel good at all. The headache seemed to worsen by the minute.

After about an hour, he needed to rest. He found a boulder to sit on and took up his binoculars to see what lay ahead. Down the beach, less than a mile away, he saw a couple and a dog walking. Alex drank some water and felt both energy and hope returning.

As he got closer, he saw some cars in a parking area close to the beach and several people walking, playing with dogs, and fishing. He reached the first couple after half an hour and greeted them.

"Good morning. Can you tell me if there is a medical clinic nearby? I fell and hit a rock, and I need to see a doctor or a nurse," he said. They looked at him like they were seeing a ghost.

The woman said, "My goodness, you look bad. We have a hospital ten miles from here; we'll take you there. Let's help you with the backpack. You've lost a lot of blood, just by looking at your clothes. Come on, we have a pickup. Maybe you can sit in the back."

Alex thanked them and offered to pay for the ride, but that was out of the question. They got to the pickup. Alex climbed up on the bed and used his backpack as a backrest.

*   *   *

Alex woke up in a bed with a nurse looking down at him. He had no idea where he was or what time it was.

"Good morning," the nurse said. "How do you feel?"

"I feel OK, thank you. But why am I in a hospital bed?"

She didn't answer him and left. A few minutes later, a doctor came in, smiling.

"Good morning, Alex. My name is Dr. Fleming. How do you feel today? You were quite messed up yesterday," the doctor said.

Alex made an attempt to sit up, but that didn't go so well.

"No, you won't be able to move for a while," the doctor said. "You lost a lot of blood, and your head wound is bad. It looks like you have been hiking for a few days with that wound. That is remarkable. What happened out there?"

"Oh, well, I stumbled and fell on a rock. I guess I didn't do a good job patching it up," Alex said. "You said 'yesterday.' Have I been here since yesterday?"

"Yes, you have, and we will keep you here for at least a couple of weeks. But you will be unwrapped and not tied down in a few days. Besides your wound, you are in pretty good shape, as far as I can see. At first, we weren't even sure you would make it. We got your wallet and ID, so we know who you are. We also found your phone, so you can call your family. We have not done that yet. Do you have any idea how far you walked since the accident? I'm only asking as a matter of medical curiosity. Most people wouldn't be able to move at all with that head injury."

Alex tried to come up with a credible answer without disclosing the whole ordeal. He couldn't come up with any. "I don't have a very clear memory. I patched up my head after the fall, then walked for maybe a mile or two. Then I slept and walked some miles again. I think I slept one more night, but it's a bit foggy. I really don't know. Maybe I hit my head harder than I thought."

"That's probably right, which only makes this thing even more remarkable. Maybe your memory will come back in the next couple of days. I must leave now, but I'll see you in a few hours. In the meantime, eat and drink as much as you can."

Dr. Fleming stood up and left the room. Alex had a feeling the friendly doctor knew more than he let on. He felt a bit like a fish on a hook.

There was a TV on the wall, and they had put the control box by his right hand. He turned the TV on and got the news: first national, then local. There was nothing about any shootings or missing boats, but at least he found out it was Friday.

A nurse came in with some pills. "These are for the inflammation on your head and left arm," she said. "The right leg is fine; we just had to clean it out. It must have been some rock you fell on!"

Again, it was a comment that made him feel that the hospital knew more and was waiting for him to come clean. But that was not in the cards—at least, not yet.

Alex was thinking—about Alina, about his family, about this whole incredible situation, and about the lack of news from all that had happened both here and in Colorado. The only explanation was that it was classified, like the entire battle had never happened. That could also mean that his own involvement never happened, which, if true, would be fantastic.

But Alina . . . she had happened, regardless of any classification. He did not believe she had been in any line of fire. She was alive, and he must find her. And here he was, lying in a hospital bed and couldn't even move his head.

*   *   *

Dr. Fleming was frustrated. That didn't happen often. When something bothered him, he addressed the issue, and it was over. Early Friday afternoon, he decided to call his old friend, Commander Hartman.

"Good afternoon, my friend. I have a simple question: Is the FBI agent I met Wednesday morning still around?"

"Yes," the commander answered, "I believe she just returned from the hospital in Seattle. She and the Russian lady, Alina, were there returning the children to their parents. I have her number."

*   *   *

Linda's phone rang. It was an unknown caller, but she still answered.

"Good afternoon, Agent Crawford. This is Dr. Fleming. We met briefly Wednesday morning at the coast guard station. I have a problem I need help with. Do you have time to talk for a few minutes?"

"Yes, and I will be happy to help if I can," Linda said.

"When I got on that vessel Tuesday evening and started to examine the children, Alina, who I also met Wednesday morning, was helping me. When I asked her if the children were on any medication, she said she didn't know the answer; she had only been on the boat for half an hour. I thought she had misunderstood my question, that her English was not that good, so I let it go. Later when I talked with her, I realized her English was as good as mine. She had not misunderstood me at all, and that suggested that she arrived on the boat together with the shooter.

"In addition to my job as a physician in the coast guard, I work at a hospital in Forks, a small town down the coast. Yesterday around noon, a couple brought a man here. He had approached them on the beach and asked for a medical clinic.

They were concerned about his condition. He was covered in blood, and they offered to drive him here. When they arrived, he was unconscious. He had lost a lot of blood and had a serious wound to his head, along with a couple of other less serious wounds. We fixed him up, and he slept until a few hours ago. When I talked to him and asked about the head wound, he said he had fallen and hit a rock when he was out hiking.

"I have my doubts about that explanation. The wound was quite smooth around the edges, not jagged like a typical wound from a fall on a rock. It looked more like a bullet had grazed his head. But there could be reasons for his response; he could have short-term memory loss, or maybe he never felt the shot in the first place if the adrenaline had dulled his senses. Then, when he discovered the wound, he thought he got it from falling and hitting something. Or he didn't want me to know how he got it, which is understandable if he believes he will be charged for killing all those people.

"In summary, I believe he is the shooter and that he and Alina know each other. I was going to ask if he knew Alina, but after his first response and his possible short-term memory loss, I decided to call you instead. His name is Alex Donner."

Linda had not said a word. Now she answered, "Thank you, Dr. Fleming. I will check and let you know."

Alina was sitting in the same room a few chairs away and had overheard what Linda had said, which was almost nothing; the doctor had done all the talking. Linda continued to be silent, trying to figure out how to break the news. She decided to ask a very simple question: "Is your partner's name Alex?"

Alina jumped up. "What happened? Is he OK?"

Linda's smile gave her the answer.

"Where is he? When can I see him?" Alina asked.

"Alex is at a hospital in Forks, about half an hour's ride by helicopter. Your friend Dr. Fleming is taking care of him, so he is in good hands. Let me find out when we can get a ride over there. And Alina, maybe you should bring your bag, just in case."

They flew down to Forks. It was a spectacularly beautiful trip with the snow-covered Mount Olympus to the left, the Strait of Juan de Fuca to the right, and the Pacific Ocean in the background. Alina smiled when she thought about traveling part of that distance in their little boat only three days ago.

They landed at the hospital. Linda asked the pilot to wait for her; she would only stay a few minutes.

Dr. Fleming met them at the door. He shook Alina's hand and thanked her for her help with the children. He was glad to see her again, and for a very different and happier reason. He led them into the hospital and down a short corridor. He knocked on a door and walked in, followed by Alina and Linda. Alex was lying in a bed. Only his face was visible. His whole head was wrapped, and he could not move it, not even an inch. But he could move his arms and eyes, and he could smile, and he could talk.

"Alex," he said, "I have a couple of friends who would like to say hi. I believe you've already met Alina, and this is Agent Crawford. She's with the FBI. They heard about your hiking mishap and just wanted to make sure we treat you well here. I'll see you all later."

Alina had already walked past him and was holding Alex's hand. That was all she dared to touch. He looked like a mummy with all the wrapping, but Dr. Fleming had told her about his expectations: Alex should be unwrapped and somewhat mobile in three to four days and fully recovered in a few weeks.

Linda shook Alex's free hand.

"I'm very glad to finally meet you, Alex. It's been a tough couple of weeks trying to keep up with you and Alina. Next time, try to move a bit slower. On a more serious note, all that happened regarding this crime is classified. No legal proceedings will come out of it, not even an investigation. I also have a personal greeting from the president to Alina and Tanya. He's inviting them to lunch at the White House. He wants to personally thank them for helping to solve this huge international kidnapping crime. That includes both citizenships and new identities, as well as a free and safe life in the US. You are also invited, Alex, as Alina's friend."

When her message had been delivered, Linda excused herself. The two of them did not need a chaperone around. Alex would be immobilized for several days anyway. He had been millimeters from death, and according to Dr. Fleming, the travel from the accident to the hospital in his condition was nothing short of a miracle.

The following morning, Dr. Fleming came to check on Alex. Alina was there; she had slept in a bed pulled in for her. He examined Alex and sat down on the only empty chair before he spoke.

"The good news is that your recovery is progressing well. You are doing fine, but we cannot rush the head wound healing. You will be here for at least two weeks. And that brings up another question for Alina. If you plan to be here for some time, we can arrange a small apartment. This is a popular summer vacation place, and the season is still a month away. Linda also told me you have a cousin in Colorado who may want to join you. If she comes, we can find a two-bedroom apartment. The FBI will pay for her travel as well as the apartment. This is all Linda's idea, so don't thank me."

Alina was already on her feet. "Oh my God, I totally forgot to call Tanya. That would be wonderful. I'll call her right away."

"Good, do that. I have some other things to talk to Alex about," Dr. Fleming said.

When Alina had left the room, he said, "Alex, I have a question for you. You have no obligation to answer, so it's really a favor I ask for. But first, some background. Besides my job here, I'm also a captain in the coast guard. This past week, I was on call and stayed at the Coast Guard Air Station in Port Angeles. They were some interesting days. On Tuesday morning, we received an alert to check all vessels leaving the US and Canada as of midnight on Tuesday. Particular attention was to be given Russian vessels. We were to look for young children being kidnapped and smuggled out. We were all busy getting ready for that undertaking—adding staff, putting resources out at various stations. I was in a helicopter group that was deployed to the Coast Guard Station at Neah Bay.

"In the middle of all that activity, at 7:04 p.m., we got a Mayday call regarding a distressed Russian vessel. The caller was on a sailboat and could not assist. Our first reaction was that it was a test to check our readiness. Regardless, we responded as efficiently as possible. I was part of the group that got to the vessel. It was definitely not a test. Five people shot dead were lying all around, and blood covered the entire superstructure and lower decks. Even for seasoned guardsmen, it was shocking. Down in the stateroom area, we found five people locked in a room. Alina was one of them. The other were three young children and the Russian consul, who had died only minutes before our arrival.

"Alina later told us that when they got into international waters, the consul, who was her uncle, had been arrested and taken prisoner. He had sabotaged Russia's kidnapping and drug smuggling operations. When Alina came on board, she was arrested as well, and both were to be prosecuted back in

Russia. They believed Alina had been part of a group that had killed several people who operated the business in the US. Her frequent communication with her uncle over the last week, in addition to being his niece, had led them to that conclusion.

"The man on the sailboat who brought her was presumably also part of that group and should be killed and drowned. Hundreds of empty shells on the vessel indicated that they indeed had tried to kill him. We don't know what happened to him, but at least we had proof that he had killed all of them.

"Early Wednesday morning, we got new instructions. By order of the president, the entire event was classified, and all involved were under witness protection. Also, the order to check all vessels was revoked because all the missing children had been found or located. The vessel was attacked five hours before our search order took effect. Without Alina's and the caller's interference, that vessel would be on its way to Russia now with Alina and the children.

"The coast guard had already started to look for the sailboat that placed the call. Being a small boat and totally shot up, it could not have traveled far. Guardsmen searched the waters all morning, and the only thing they found was a life ring floating about twenty miles south of Cape Flattery. Any boat could have lost that. The name on the ring was *Springtime*. We believe the boat has sunk from all the shots. The coast guard has several reasons to find the boat. Lying at the bottom, it can be a trap for fishing nets and anchors, and it can also leak fuel. From what I understand, you were hiking somewhere up the coast. Did you see or hear anything that can help us locate that boat?"

Alex had already shut his eyes. He didn't want the doctor to see any reaction. After considering this new information for a minute, he looked up at him.

"The boat sank about one mile from land, approximately five miles north of the parking area where I got the ride. I pulled the dinghy into the vegetation where I landed, so that would be the best indicator. It shouldn't be too hard to find. Now, how can I get my hands on that life ring?" Alex smiled, and so did Dr. Fleming.

Moments later, Alina came back after her call to Tanya. With no words floating in the air, she immediately started to fill the void.

"Tanya is so happy. She'll come here as soon as she can get a flight. Linda had already told her all the good news about the children, our citizenship, and this whole nightmare being over. She was taken care of by Dr. Black for a week through the most difficult drug withdrawal period. It had not been that hard at all."

Alex listened, but he also had a question. "That's really good to hear, but what's the news about the children?"

Alina and Dr. Fleming looked at each other. This was all classified. Could they share it with Alex? Dr. Fleming decided they could.

"There has been some development while you were out hiking and having a good time. But I think you are bound by the confidentiality agreement as well, so here is the very short version of what transpired. Based on all the evidence, a call was made by our president to President Lenkov this past Wednesday. Lenkov was unaware of any kidnappings and promised the children back. Alina got a list from her uncle with the names and whereabouts of the six children that already had been shipped to Russia, which she gave to Linda. Also, Alina and Linda have returned the three children on the vessel to their parents. Too bad you were out hiking and couldn't be part of this incredible event."

Now all of them smiled.

The following day, a cool and sunny Sunday, Tanya arrived in Seattle. She was met by a coast guard officer and taken by a waiting helicopter to Fork. There she was met by Dr. Fleming and Alina. The two cousins moved into a nice, sunny, two-bedroom apartment within walking distance of the hospital. Alina spent all her waking hours with Alex, while Tanya walked and biked around and beyond the little town. That did not go unnoticed by the unmarried Dr. Fleming. On Thursday, he invited Tanya to dinner. After all, they were both going to eat, so why not?

Three weeks later, Alex was almost back to normal and was discharged from the small hospital. He decided to stay in town for another couple of weeks in the apartment with Alina and Tanya. They all started to hike around the beautiful Olympic National Park, sometimes accompanied by Dr. Fleming.

Alex's calls to his daughters were a bit complicated. Yes, he had a wonderful time in the mountains. After a few weeks, the snow had started to melt, so he had switched to hiking. One day, he went to buy some fresh food at a supermarket in Eagle. There, he got into a conversation with a Russian woman named Alina. She needed some help with her shopping. She was on her way to Seattle to hike the Olympic National Park. After a lot of talking and lunch, he had decided to join her. They were having a great time in the park, and he had invited her back to Breckenridge. They should get there by mid-May, and Alina looked forward to meeting them all.

It was the truth—maybe not the whole truth, but close enough considering all the classifications.

Chapter 22

The government wheels move slowly, if they move at all, except when they move fast. Or *very* fast. Linda flew home on Sunday. On Monday, she asked her office to check a name: Alex Donner. Dr. Fleming had given her Alex's full name and indicated that he was in his sixties. He obviously didn't see that as a breach of doctor-patient confidentiality. Linda had a nagging hunch and needed to know.

On Tuesday, she got her answer. It was a long report with lots of names, dates, and addresses. She scanned it for the essentials. Mr. Alex Donner was a resident of Breckenridge, Colorado. He was a widower for eight years and had two grown and married daughters, one living in Evergreen, Colorado, with three children, and one in Littleton, Colorado, with a five-year-old son.

Linda had her confirmation, but just for fun, she looked at the street address in Littleton. It bordered on a park with a playground—the same playground where a five-year-old boy had been abducted three weeks ago.

And some people don't believe in coincidences.

*   *   *

The data center in the storage room was a treasure trove. It took on a life of its own. The volume of information hidden in it required a small army of technicians, analysts, and back-office staff for sorting and filing, not so much for future historians as for present and anxious law enforcement officers. The entire "not-for-profit" company proved exceedingly profitable.

Lawyers did not need much time to conclude that the classification agreement with Russia only covered the kidnapping side of this crime empire. No one opposed that conclusion. Everything else was open for prosecution.

Hundreds of names with addresses and millions of dollars from drug smuggling, gun smuggling, human trafficking, and other crimes were neatly listed and accounted for. Law enforcement had never before gotten so much evidence served on a huge silver platter. People all over the US and Canada from all walks of life were quickly and quietly picked up and locked up. Most of them had the same reaction. It was supposed to be under the radar, guaranteed untraceable. Was it all a government sting?

There were many questions and no answers.

*   *   *

The White House lunch for Alex, Alina, and Tanya took place in late June. Alex was fully recovered, and his hair had grown long enough to cover a rather long and deep scar on his head. Among the guests were Director Wrangler, Agent Baker, Agent Callahan, Agent Crawford, Dr. Lopez, Dr. Fleming, and their spouses, all good friends of Tanya, Alina, and Alex. Two unusually excited ladies were sworn in as US citizens by the president in person.

After the ceremony, they ate an excellent lunch in a small dining room with an informal and relaxed atmosphere. The weather was as good as can be in early summer in DC. The president suggested they take their coffee in the Rose Garden.

When they were seated with their coffee cups, the president stood up to say a few words.

"The problem with the classification of this entire kidnapping nightmare, which is part of our deal with President Lenkov, is that the people who have done the job and cleared up the mess cannot be properly recognized and rewarded. Not for thirty years, and who will remember anything then?

"The highest civil honor in our country, the Presidential Medal of Freedom, is now part of the classified documentation and will be given to the recipient thirty years down the road or to the family if that person has checked out. I just want you to know, Alex, because your name is on the medal. And maybe you want to prepare your grandson, Mike, who will be thirty-five then, by writing a book or something. You have thirty years to think about it.

"We don't know everything that happened out there when that crime empire was taken down, but we do know two things: that you put your life on the line and that you saved eleven children who would otherwise have been lost forever. My sincere thanks on behalf of the entire country, and our congratulations, Alex."

The President and First Lady shook his hand and then applauded with the other. Alex didn't say a word. He couldn't find a word to say.